THE CHERRY VALLEY MIDDLE SCHOOL NEWS

DEAR KNOW-IT-ALL!

★ ★ ★

Cast Your Ballot!

by RACHEL WISE

Simon Spotlight

New York London Toronto Sydney New Delhi

This book is a work of fiction. Any references to historical events, real people, or real places are used fictitiously. Other names, characters, places, and events are products of the author's imagination, and any resemblance to actual events or places or persons, living or dead, is entirely coincidental.

SIMON SPOTLIGHT

An imprint of Simon & Schuster Children's Publishing Division
1230 Avenue of the Americas, New York, New York 10020
Copyright © 2013 by Simon & Schuster, Inc. All rights reserved, including the right of reproduction in whole or in part in any form.
SIMON SPOTLIGHT and colophon are registered trademarks of Simon & Schuster, Inc.
Text by Elizabeth Doyle Carey
Designed by Bob Steimle

For information about special discounts for bulk purchases, please contact Simon & Schuster Special Sales at 1-866-506-1949 or business@simonandschuster.com.
Manufactured in the United States of America 0713 OFF
First Edition 10 9 8 7 6 5 4 3 2 1
ISBN 978-1-4424-8792-5 (pbk)
ISBN 978-1-4424-8793-2 (hc)
ISBN 978-1-4424-8794-9 (eBook)
Library of Congress Control Number 2013940630

Chapter 1

POLLS A PROVING GROUND FOR RISING STAR REPORTER

★ ★ ★

It is election season at Cherry Valley Middle School, and I cannot *wait* to cover it for our school newspaper, the *Cherry Valley Voice*. Everyone pays attention to the news around election time, so I'm really psyched to be in the middle of it. Plus, it's good training ground for when I get older and am a star reporter covering the presidential election somewhere (watch for me!). I am obsessed with journalism and have spent years reading posts, blogs, newspapers, and magazines and watching coverage of real elections on TV, and I am *ready* to get in there and do it myself! I can just see the headline: ***Polls a Proving Ground for Rising Star Reporter.***

Elections have it all: person-on-the-street interviews, polls, background digging, daily highs and
lows, analysis—the best stuff journalism has to
offer. And what's great is I'll get to do it all–and
under my own byline, Sam Martone. Oh, along with
that of my writing partner and the crush of my life,
Michael Lawrence. Michael and I make a good
writing team. Luckily, the paper's faculty supervi-
sor, Mr. Trigg, agrees, so he partners us up for most
stories. I have to say, we do make a great pair.

Today Mr. Trigg announced in our newspaper
staff meeting that we'd begin election coverage
for the next issue. Everyone began whispering
with their neighbor (Michael was late, as usual,
so I didn't have a neighbor to whisper with at that
exact moment), and Mr. Trigg had to call us all to
order again.

"Wonderful enthusiasm here today!" He
chuckled. "Nothing like an election to get the
journalistic juices flowing! All right, then, let's
talk assignments. Nikil Gupta and Niall Carey,
how about a piece on the election process here
at Cherry Valley Middle? Let's focus on: How do

people get nominated? How do the campaigns work? Where and how do we vote?"

Mr. Trigg looked at his notes, and just then, Michael entered with a sheepish grin. He nodded at Mr. Trigg apologetically and quickly joined me on the love seat just inside the newsroom door. I always grab this seat early and save him the other half—it's the best seat for late arrivals, which is what Michael always is. Plus, it *is* called a *love* seat, right? Swoon!

"Ah, Mr. Lawrence. So glad you could join us today," said Mr. Trigg, peering at Michael over his reading glasses. Michael is one of Mr. Trigg's favorites since he's an amazing writer and has a photographic memory, so Mr. Trigg lets Michael get away with a lot of other stuff, like lateness. "I'd like you and Ms. Martone to do profiles of the candidates for school president. Front-page stories. Lots of background, person-on-the-street, and primary interviews with the candidates. Okay, you two?"

He looked at us, and we nodded vigorously and smiled. This was a plum assignment. It would be fun to research and write, and we'd get to work together, which wasn't always a given. I was ecstatic.

"The two candidates are John Scott and . . ." He looked down at his notes. "It's here somewhere . . . hiding . . . I wouldn't want to be running against John Scott either! Oh, here it is! Anthony Wright. Okay?"

"Got it," I said, writing their names down in my trusty notebook even though of course I knew already. I had been reading a lot of posts about who was running, and paying attention for weeks already.

"Good note-taking, Pasty," whispered Michael.

I nodded, happy enough to ignore his nickname for me for the millionth time, as well as the fact that he always teases me for writing things down in my notebook.

Mr. Trigg continued. "Let us all remember, reporters, that we are impartial. As the press, we merely reflect what the public says, and we strive to be the ultimate in fair and accurate reporting, especially when it comes to elections. Now, opinion pieces are a different matter, but I don't know that we'll be using them this time around. Feelings *do* get hurt," said Mr. Trigg, rolling his eyes heavenward. "In the words of the late, great Winston Churchill, 'There is no such thing as public opinion. There is only published opinion.' Too true, dear Winston, too true," he said, shaking his head sadly.

Everyone giggled, since Mr. Trigg has this unbelievable ability to find the perfect Churchill quotation for anything. Everyone makes bets on how many times Trigger will mention Churchill in a meeting. Some kids even think he makes the quotations up. I always write them down because I like them, so I'm here to say they're all real because I've Googled them! I actually think they'd make a great article one day.

After the meeting Michael and I both had to run to classes, but we made a plan to meet up later and brainstorm.

"Who are you voting for, by the way?" he asked, a twinkle in his eye.

"I am a journalist! I am objective!" I said indignantly. "I won't know until I have all the facts and can make an informed decision!"

"Innocent until proven guilty, then?" he teased with that adorable smile of his.

"Of course," I huffed, but I smiled back. How could I not?

At lunch I ate with my best friend, Hailey Jones, and our friends Kristen and Jenna. We are going to the movies this Friday and out for pizza at Slices, and we wanted to talk about which movie to see.

"Action is where it's at, my friends," declared Hailey. She wanted us to go see a movie about a spaceship that loses control or something.

"Uh, nothing personal, Hails, but you know that's not really my bag," I said.

Hailey rolled her eyes as she took another bite of her usual lunch: white rice with salt and butter (yes, it's kind of gross, and yes, Hailey's mother would not be happy if she knew that's what she ate most days). She said, "You just want to go to one of those old-fashioned Jane Austen novel movies or talky-talky movies you like. I just can't sit still for that!"

Kristen and Jenna were used to Hailey's and my battling over details, but everyone knows that underneath it all we're best friends.

"Well, I have to be true to myself," I said, all fake righteous.

"So do I! I just want to kick back, relax, and get scared!"

Everyone laughed, as Hailey had intended, and she smiled a lopsided grin. I didn't want to propose a vote because I knew Jenna and Kristen wanted to see the same movie about old-fashioned times that I did, and it wouldn't be fair to gang up on Hailey. We'd just have to let the movie times decide what we saw and never mind accounting for people's interests.

"Oh, and by the way, there will be way more cute boys at my movie than yours!" said Hailey in one last attempt.

"Hmm. You have a point," I had to admit. "But any cute boys in particular?" These three girls all know about my huge crush on Michael.

Hailey's eyes twinkled. "We could invite him!"

"No. It's a girls' night," I said firmly. We'd been planning on this date for weeks. Not that I would really have the nerve to invite him anyway.

Or maybe I would. Would that be weird? I realized they were all looking at me. "Anyway, I'm not going to base my activities on Michael Lawrence's interests!" I declared.

"Famous last words!" Hailey laughed.

"Humph," I said. "Let's change the subject. What do you all know about the candidates for school president?"

"Ooh, John Scott is sooo cute!" said Jenna.

"Majorly," agreed Kristen.

"Hails?" I asked.

"He's cute, I guess. But I didn't know we were voting on looks alone," she said.

"That's my girl!" I cheered. "Good answer!"

"Not that I know anything about the other guy," she said.

"Who is the other guy?" asked Kristen.

"Anthony Wright," I said, shrugging a little.

"No, but who *is* he?" asked Jenna.

"Yeah, I know what you mean," I agreed. "Pretty low on the radar."

"Like, invisible." Kristen nodded.

"I've got to write profiles on both of them for

the next issue of the *Voice*, so I'll know a lot more very soon," I said.

"Need an assistant for the Scott interview?" joked Jenna.

"I already have one!" I declared. And, spotting Michael across the cafeteria, I said, "And he's right there!"

"Old lover boy himself," teased Hailey.

Here are some of the reasons I love Michael: He is tall and in very good shape from being on the football and baseball teams. He has dark hair with bright blue eyes, which is a great combo, and dimples. He is a good dresser—lots of flannel shirts and khakis—but it's not just the way he looks. He also has nice manners, and he's an excellent writer and a talented cook.

Michael and I mostly get along very well, but we sometimes fight, and I hate that. I want him to always like me, and I want for us to always get along, but when things aren't right, I have to stand up for myself and to him, no matter what. It's just the way I am. I might compromise on some things, but I won't change just to make someone like me.

Remembering my responsibilities, I snapped out of my love-struck dream. There was something I needed to grab from the newsroom, and now would be a good time.

"Okay, chicas, I'm off," I said, gathering up my tray and my messenger bag.

"So soon?" said Hailey.

"Yes, but I'll meet you after school," I said. I usually help Hailey with her homework if I have free time. She's dyslexic and she has a school-appointed tutor, but only one or two days a week. I help the rest of the time, since she hates reading and writing and I love it.

"Later!" called Kristen and Jenna.

I walked a few steps away and looked up and there was Michael, standing with his lunch tray. "Leaving so soon?" he asked.

Darn it!

"Uh, yes . . . ?" I stammered.

"Can't you stay for a minute?" he asked.

I sighed. I'd love nothing more, but what I needed to do couldn't wait. "I'm sorry. I just can't," I said.

Michael sighed now too. "Okay. Maybe later?"

"I have to help Hailey with her homework after school," I said. "Can we talk by phone tonight? Or . . . ?" I was hoping he'd ask me to meet him after school again like he did a few weeks ago.

"Sure. Or maybe we can get together tomorrow," he said.

Yesss!

Michael did a U-turn away from where he'd been heading (toward my table!) and scanned the crowd for his guy friends.

"Great," I said. "Sorry to miss you today."

"Yup," he agreed. "Bye."

"Bye."

Parting is such sweet sorrow, as Shakespeare liked to say. *Oh well. Business is business*, I thought, and I headed back to the newsroom.

Chapter 2

JOURNALIST BUSTED IN LOCKED OFFICE CRACKS UNDER QUESTIONING

★ ★ ★

Back at the newsroom, I tried the handle to find that the door was locked. I could see through the opaque glass in the door that the lights were out, too. *Good*, I thought. It was just how I like it.

Looking quickly over my shoulder in both directions, I slid my key into the lock, opened the door, slipped inside, and swiftly shut and locked it behind me. *Phew!* So far so good. Only Mr. Trigg, the editor in chief, and I have keys to the office, and only two of us know why I'm there. So I'm pretty safe.

I took a deep breath; then I got my next key ready to open my mailbox.

Suddenly, there was a rattling at the door.

Someone was trying to come in! I froze right in the middle of the room. Should I hide? Act like I fell asleep on the love seat? What?

Journalist Busted in Locked Office Cracks Under Questioning.

Oh no.

But the person gave up and went away.

I resumed my creep to the mailbox and was just putting my key into the lock when I heard someone at the door again. This time, a key entered the lock neatly and the door opened. If it was the editor in chief, I was toast! I held my breath, nowhere to hide, nothing to mask what I was doing.

Whew, what a relief! But oh boy, thank goodness it was just Mr. Trigg. He flicked the lights on and startled when he saw me.

"Goodness, Ms. Martone, you gave me a fright!"

"Likewise," I said with a relieved grin. "Would you mind shutting the door for a minute?" I gestured at my mailbox.

"Oh, certainly! So sorry! Of course. And I'll turn the lights out, as it was, okeydoke?" he began to whisper. "Like Woodward and Bernstein in here!"

I giggled at the reference to the two reporters whose top-secret investigation of election tactics brought down President Nixon. Mr. Trigg loves the cloak-and-dagger aspects of my other job at the paper, which is that I am the top-secret advice columnist who writes as "Dear Know-It-All." If my identity is ever discovered, I lose my job, so the anonymity is something I work hard to maintain. Thus all the sneaking around.

I quickly opened my mailbox and withdrew the three paltry letters inside, as Mr. Trigg put a finger to his lips and tiptoed to his office. I locked the mailbox back up and went to the door to unlock it and turn on the light while simultaneously jamming the letters down into my messenger bag and out of sight.

Sighing in relief, I crossed the newsroom to Mr. Trigg's office in the corner. A little bit of Fleet Street right in our very midst, it was decked in Union Jacks and Churchill posters, with a double-decker-bus pencil sharpener, a

Keep Calm and Carry On poster, and other common British accoutrements, including a small electric teakettle, which he was just setting on to boil.

"Fancy a spot of tea?" he asked me.

"No thanks. I just had lunch."

"Anything good in the mail?" he asked, wiggling his eyebrows up and down.

I smiled. "I don't know yet. I can't really check here. I'd hate to get caught."

"Very professional. Impressive as always. I'll certainly make a note of that in your file."

"My file? What file?"

Mr. Trigg looked at me in confusion. "I have files on all my writers and editors. I keep their clips in there, notes about their style, work, impressive judgment calls, all that sort of thing."

"Why?" I asked incredulously.

Mr. Trigg looked back at me, equally incredulous. "References, applications, background checks. People ask me all the time for help with those things."

"Applications? Like to college?"

"Certainly. And some to private high schools or even boarding schools. My editors and writers often apply as journalists for summer internships or jobs just out of school, and they want me to write their recommendations."

"Huh. Seems like they're stretching back in time pretty far. Sixth grade? Eighth grade?"

"You'd be surprised how short it seems to me," he said, pouring his hot water over his tea bag. "In any case, I can easily tell what my students' fundamental characters are at this stage, their work ethic, their punctuality, attention to detail. There are quite a few character traits that don't change over time."

"Wow. I guess I'd better be nicer to you," I joked.

"Don't change a thing," he said, smiling warmly over the rim of his mug as he took a tentative sip. "Incidentally, most newspapers keep files on famous people. Used to be clippings; now I'm sure it's all digitized. It helped when reporters needed to do a story on someone notable. They'd just order up the file and have plenty of info to get started. Also used it for obituaries, of course. But mostly very handy for business and politics."

"I guess now we just Google," I said.

"Of course. But Googling is not as good in some ways. It pulls up too much stuff, things that might be irrelevant or out of context, and then it doesn't pull up some of the good stuff, like old profiles with analysis."

"Hmm," I said. "I'll remember that."

"Good. Now, anything else going on?"

"Not at the moment!" I looked at my watch. "Except I have my next class in about two minutes! Gotta run."

"Cheerio, Ms. Martone," he said as I turned to leave.

"Bye!"

I raced to make my next class on time, my messenger bag thumping my leg as I ran, and all I could think about was *Imagine: Mr. Trigg is already thinking about me going to college one day!*

★   ★   ★

That night, after Hailey had left and my mom and my sister and I had finished our dinner (fajita night!), I finally had five minutes to myself to sit at my desk and open my Dear Know-It-All letters. They usually come in along certain themes each time, and these were no exception.

There was the "my family doesn't understand me" letter, on plain notebook paper in a white business envelope:

Dear Know-It-All,

My mom is always hounding me to clean my room, but I like it the way it is. I don't see it as messy just because I have my things around and some snacks in there. Why should I have to clean it to her specifications?

From,

Messy with Style

Hmm. I guess if your mom is paying the bills (including the exterminator bill), Messy, then you have to obey her standards. Find another form of self-expression.

Next, there was the "homework's getting me down" letter, on camp stationery from a boys' camp in Maine.

Dear Know-It-All

When do we get a break I'm busy all summer with programs and camps and then busy all year with homework and studying for tests When do I get a chance to sleep late and lie around if I want

WHEN

Signed,

Tired

Wow. Too tired even to punctuate. Well, I hear you, Tired, and the answer is never, I think. I'm sorry.

Finally, the third letter was a "love hurts" letter, on pink scalloped stationery, of course, with a matching envelope.

Dear Know-It-All,

I like an eighth grader (I'm in sixth), but he won't even look at me. Do I stand a chance? If so, what can I do to get him to like me?

Signed,

Adoring Underclassperson

Hmm. A tough one. My short answer to that would be: An eighth grader will never like a sixth grader because that is just totally uncool. Maybe in a few years, when age doesn't matter as much, but probably not too soon.

None of these letters was the juicy, meaty kind of letter I liked. I was disappointed but not surprised. Often I'll get batch after batch of tired clichés and I'll get discouraged. I don't want to print the same thing over and over, even though this is clearly what's on everyone's mind. I like things that inspire some debate or make people think.

Columnist Solves World's Problems One Kid at a Time.

Ha! As if!

Well, I still have some time before the next issue is due, I thought. Something will come up. It always does. And sometimes I'll get, like, four really good letters and have an impossible time choosing. My mom calls it "feast or famine." I know what she means.

I hid the letters in my new Know-It-All hiding spot, behind my headboard. My sister, Allie, is very snoopy, and more than once, I've caught her in here where she could have stumbled upon my trove of letters. I can't risk it because she is a major blab-bermouth. If she found out I'm Know-It-All, I'd lose my job and be ruined.

It was time to wrap up my homework, but I couldn't resist a little Googling.

First I looked for information on John Scott, the school presidential candidate. It was unfortunate that he had such a common name. Tons of stuff came up, and it was nearly impossible to wade through. Sure there were obvious things I could weed out, like I knew he hadn't robbed a bank, but I couldn't be sure that it wasn't him who'd had his bike stolen from the Cherry Valley mall last year, or who'd saved a little girl from drowning at the town beach. I began to yearn for the days of Mr. Trigg's clipping files.

Anthony Wright wasn't much better. It was definitely him who'd won the state chess championship, because I remember seeing the massive trophy in the lobby at school. I didn't even recognize him in the picture (waaaay under the radar), but nothing bad came up about him, and I couldn't wade through the sea of other Anthony Wrights (Fighting off muggers! Winning the lottery! Heading off to Iraq!) to find more.

I made a note to search the back issues of the *Cherry Valley Voice* as a start and packed it in for the night.

Chapter 3
COWRITERS COMPETE FOR EXCLUSIVE INTERVIEW

★ ★ ★

I cannot even pretend to like coffee, even though it's considered cool to drink it and most journalists live on it. I wish I did like it. It's just that I find it so untasty, I can't even have a tiny bit to try and get used to it. Not that Mom would even let me. She has a strict "no coffee" rule for us—even decaf—although I know for a fact Allie drinks it when she's with her friends.

Anyway, Michael likes it, which makes me kind of like him even more. It's like he's mature and manly enough to tolerate the stuff, even if he does put in lots of cream and sugar. That's what I discovered the one other time we hung out at the Java Stop. Today I ordered a hot chocolate, just to be sociable, but I did feel a tiny bit embarrassed and babyish doing it. Especially when he grinned at me in that teasing way he has and said, "Can't handle the strong stuff?"

Aaargh!

"Coffee makes me jittery. I'm hyper enough as it is," I said, and that made him pipe down.

We found a table near the front, and I was privately thrilled that anyone walking by—or in and out—could see me sitting there with gorgeous Michael Lawrence. I wanted this moment to last forever. At least, until I spilled my hot chocolate and got some on Michael's pants and had to pat him down with flimsy brown recycled napkins. Oh boy. He swore I didn't burn him and that it was nice to smell like chocolate.

New hot chocolate in hand, table dried, pants blotted, and notebooks out, we finally got down to business.

"Okay, Spilly," said Michael. "How should we divide this up?"

Michael likes to make up new nicknames for me all the time, based on whatever klutzy or dorky thing I've just done (so, besides Pasty, I have Trippy, Listy, Snacky, and most recently, Spilly).

I took a long, patient breath and began. "Why don't we each take a candidate to research? Internet, *Cherry Valley Voice*, school yearbooks— even from elementary—other kids. Then we'll both interview them . . . together?"

But Michael was shaking his head. "I like splitting up the research. But we shouldn't both interview them at the same time. Let's meet them separately. That way . . ."

I was already nodding. I knew where he was going with this. "We can see if we had the same reactions."

Now Michael was nodding. "Exactly!"

We smiled at each other in blissful agreement. But wait, with that settled, was our coffee hour over?

I scrambled to stretch it out. "And . . . uh . . . *then*, we can—"

Michael cocked his head and listened politely, as if I might have some fabulous idea to add, which of course, I didn't! Unless Michael did?

"Do one of our famous . . . ," he interrupted.

"Buddybook polls!" we both shouted at the same time.

Michael put his hand out for a high five. "Good one, Spilly!" he said.

I made a note in my notebook that we'd do a poll, and Michael grinned at me as I wrote. "Still writing everything down in your book?" he asked.

"I don't have your photographic memory. We've been through this before."

"No, I get it. Different people have different styles. It took me a while to get yours, but now I wouldn't want you to change a thing."

I was pleased but squirmed uncomfortably. "Thank you, I think," I said kind of gruffly, to mask my happiness.

Click! A flash went off, and I turned, blinking, to see who it was.

"Hey, guys, mind if I crash your date?" said Jeff Perry, sitting down without waiting for our reply. Jeff is one of Michael's best friends, and he's the photographer for the paper, too. He always has his camera.

"What's with the photo?" asked Michael, kind of annoyed.

"Just practicing for the campaign trail." Jeff shrugged. "I'm hoping to catch our candidates at an awkward moment. Makes great news."

Michael and I exchanged an uncomfortable look.

"Uh, like what kind of awkward moment?" I asked.

"You know, kissing a girl, stealing something, leaving the scene of an accident . . . ," said Jeff wistfully.

Michael laughed. "Seriously? You think John Scott and Anthony Wright might do any of those things?"

Jeff smiled. "I sure hope so!"

"Jeff, that is too much. The *Cherry Valley Voice* isn't a tabloid, you know," I said in my most disapproving voice. "Even in the unlikely event you snapped such an enlightening photo, Mr. Trigg would never run it."

"Hey, you never know!" said Jeff. "Anyway, I could always put it on Buddybook. So, have you guys done any digging yet? Know anything about these guys? I know John a little, from numerics class. He makes me laugh. This one time . . ."

Jeff launched into a story about John Scott that *was* pretty funny; I wished he'd leave me and Michael alone, though. Michael laughed at the end, and he and Jeff agreed that John had a good reputation as a funny guy. A tiny part of me was looking forward to meeting John.

"So, should we just send them each e-mails tonight to set up our interviews?" I asked Michael.

He nodded. "Yup. I've actually got their contact info here; I got it from the school directory. I'll send it to you."

"Wow, very organized!" I said, impressed.

"Hey, you don't have the monopoly on organization around here!" said Michael.

Another compliment!

"I know. I know . . ."

"Hey!" interrupted Jeff. "There's Anthony Wright on the coffee line now! Anthony!" he called. And when Anthony turned, Jeff snapped his photo, leaving Anthony blinking, confused, and visibly unnerved.

"Jeff, you've got to stop doing that to people.

It's really annoying!" admonished Michael.

"You know what, I'm going to go over there and introduce myself," I said. "Otherwise he's going to lump me in with you. The photo stalker!" I stood and headed across the room toward Anthony.

Anthony Wright is tall and thin with glasses. He has close-cropped curly hair and he's a plain dresser. No-name blue polo shirt, generic jeans, plain sneakers. He was nervous and kind of nerdy, though, and when I approached him, he looked over his shoulder to see if I was making my way toward someone else.

I introduced myself, and he said in a formal way, "Hello, Samantha. It's nice to meet you." Anthony's voice was deep and warm, which surprised me. I wasn't expecting it. The guy could do voice-overs for commercials if he wanted; it was that good. A little bit of his nerdiness melted away as I listened to him speak.

"So I'm going to be e-mailing you to see if I can interview you for the school paper," I said.

"Excellent. About the election?"

I nodded. "Yup. Pretty exciting stuff."

"I know," he agreed, warming up and losing a little more of his nerdiness. "There are so many things I'd like to work on. Hey, you aren't free now by any chance, are you? I have fifteen minutes until my carpool picks me up here. Do you want to talk here?"

Oh. Awkward. I didn't know what to say. Should I ditch Michael and take this opportunity? It might be better to have him be spontaneous than rehearsed. But there was Michael, waiting for me at the table. And I hadn't done any research yet on Anthony at all. Well, that sealed it.

"Actually, that's so nice of you, but I'm here with my friends . . . or friend, really. The nice one, without the camera? And also, I haven't had time to do any research on you yet, so maybe it's better . . ."

"I understand. Totally. That's fine. Just e-mail me and we'll set it up," he said. And then it was his turn to order. "Nice to meet you," he said to me, and he turned to the barista.

"Okay, bye. Thanks." I made my way back to my table, unable to shake the feeling that I'd just missed an opportunity. I sat down quietly, lost in thought, as Michael and Jeff chatted on about this week's football game. If anything, Anthony Wright just seemed awkward at first and maybe more mature than us, almost like a mini adult. I bet if you talked to him for a while, you'd forget the awkwardness and the nerdiness altogether. I rely on first impressions a lot, but Mom always tells me to give people a chance; what you see right away isn't always what you get.

"Hey. How was he?" asked Michael.

"What? Oh, really nice. Not at all the nerd I'd figured him to be, actually," I admitted.

"Sam!" Michael pointed a finger at me. "You, of all people! Judging a book by its cover!"

I laughed. "I know. Shame on me. He even offered to let me interview him right now, and I turned him down for you two clowns."

"Wait, what?" asked Michael, doing an incredulous double take. "A candidate offered an off-the-cuff interview, all access, and you said no?"

My stomach dropped. "Um, is that bad?"

Michael turned, wide-eyed, to Jeff; then they both looked back at me and nodded. "I'll say," said Michael. "I don't think an opportunity like that comes along every day." Jeff shook his head in agreement.

"Oh. Well, I wasn't prepared, so . . . I just figured it would be a waste of time."

Michael stood up. "Maybe I'll go interview him, then," he declared.

Cowriters Compete for Exclusive Interview.

"Seriously?" I asked. I couldn't believe this! I turned down Anthony to hang out with Michael, and now Michael was turning me down to hang out with Anthony! And what did that make me? That made *me* the nerd in all this, that's for sure.

"Yeah, sorry to ditch you, Paste. Do you want to join me? Or wait for me?"

I stood up now, too, embarrassed and a little offended. "No, that's all right. I'll just head home. Tons of homework, you know." I could barely meet Michael's eye.

"I guess I'm out too, then," said Jeff, standing.

"All right. Check ya later," said Michael, and he crossed the room to shake hands with Anthony Wright.

"See ya, Pasty," said Jeff outside.

"Don't call me that!" I snarled, and I set off for home.

The heels of my boots clomped as they struck the pavement. I was basically stomping home, but I was so upset, it felt good. I couldn't believe Michael had ditched our "date" for work. I couldn't believe I'd had such poor journalistic instincts that I'd rejected a really good offer for an exclusive interview so I could hang out with Michael. Who dumped me for the interview. And I couldn't believe I'd prejudged Anthony Wright so badly. I couldn't believe how annoying Jeff Perry was. I felt like kicking myself, boot heels and all. I get so mad when I think I do dumb things. I turned the corner of Buttermilk Lane and ran the rest of the way, then stormed up to my room and semi-slammed the door. Inside, I flung off my messenger bag and punched my pillow. A lot. It actually made me feel better. After a while, I took some deep breaths and began to try to talk some sense into myself (I am, after all, a professional advice giver).

Inhale: Okay, it was never a date. It was a work meeting with Michael. I shouldn't have read into it.

Exhale.

Inhale: I wasn't prepared to meet with Anthony and I would have had to interview him again anyway, and it would have looked bad.

Exhale.

Inhale: I hadn't necessarily prejudged Anthony. I'd just pieced together a logical inference based on what I knew of him already.

Exhale.

Inhale: Jeff Perry *is* annoying. Everyone thinks so.

Exhale.

Just as I was starting to feel a little calmer, my IM pinged and it was Hailey.

Scary movie Friday 7 pm. Jane Austen 4 pm or 10 pm. Ha!

Nuts! Now I was annoyed all over again!

Chapter 4

PSYCHIC FRIEND DRIVES GIRL BATTY

★ ★ ★

I was so annoyed that all I could do that night was homework. I didn't even check my e-mail or anything. When I woke up early the next day, I read my usual news feeds and blogs and stuff, and then I opened my e-mail to send an interview request each to John Scott and Anthony Wright.

But there were a few very interesting e-mails in my in-box. One was from Michael. It said:

Paste,

I'm sorry I ran off on you. I felt terrible after. A nose for news should never mean ditching your friends. Your instincts were better. Anthony wasn't all that prepared either, so it was kind of a waste of time. Nice guy, though. Will compare notes after you meet him and conduct a much-better-prepared interview than I did. Sorry if I made you doubt your instincts and manners (not to flatter myself; I probably didn't). I'd like to make it up to you. Hot-chocolate date?

M

Wait . . . did he say date? I sighed happily in my chair. A three-fer! An apology and date offer from Michael, a vindication of my noninterviewing instinct, and a confirmation of my good first impression of Anthony Wright. It couldn't get any better than this.

The next e-mail was a forward from Mr. Trigg. He mans the e-mail submissions for Dear Know-It-All—first he reads them, and if they're okay, he forwards them to me. I had an incident where someone cyber-stalked me last year while Mr. Trigg was away, so now he controls all the Internet access to the writers at the paper.

I read the forwarded e-mail, then sat back to mull it over. It said:

Dear Know-It-All,

My parents say I should be taking all these particular classes and doing only certain extracurricular activities that will help me get into college one day. The only problem is, I'm not interested in the stuff they want me to do, and the stuff I want to do, they say is a waste of time! (By the way, I'm only in seventh grade.)

What should I do? Suck it up and do these boring activities that they want me to do, or refuse? And when do I get to do what I want to do?

Signed,

College Reject Already

At first glance it was kind of a boring letter. I thought, *Reject: You're too young to worry about college; next case.* But then it occurred to me that this was a letter I could turn into a bigger message, the way I liked and what the column was really supposed to be about. The way that got everyone at Cherry Valley talking when they read my column. This was a letter about being true to yourself. In fact, just being yourself. Sure, we all need to work hard and think about the future, but to ruin your life right now and suffer hard for the future? Well, it wasn't good.

I tapped out a quick reply to Mr. Trigg to thank him for the forward; then I printed the e-mail, filed it behind my headboard, and deleted the original.

Finally there was an e-mail from John Scott, of all people. I had e-mailed him asking when he would be available for an interview. It said:

Dear Samantha,

I am excited to hear that you're covering me for the Voice. I have loved your articles on Pay to Play and school lunches and think that your coverage is fair and smart. I am available for a meeting between eleven and twelve on Wednesday and Friday, and I can also talk by phone (see number below).

Looking forward to hearing from you.

Best regards,

John Scott

Wow! He'd done his homework. I was flattered.

I fired back an e-mail making a plan to meet him for lunch on Friday and made a mental note to stop by the library to review the newspaper's archives ahead of time.

So much accomplished already today and it was only seven thirty a.m. It was going to be an awesome day! In a great mood, I even replied to Hailey:

Scary movie it is. Pizza first.

At school, things just kept getting better. I ran into Anthony Wright first thing and apologized for not being free to chat yesterday. He said he understood and that we should plan a meeting time, but we struggled for a bit to find an opening when we'd both be free. With the article due next week, I didn't want to waste any time. It turned out the only time we could both meet was Friday at five, back at the Java Stop. I'd have just enough time to run home after school, change for my night out, interview Anthony, and meet the other girls at Slices before the movie. Anthony thanked me profusely for my flexibility in planning the meeting with him after school on a Friday, but I waved it off. "It's fine," I said.

Then I saw Michael, who was so sweet and apologetic and asked me to save him a seat at lunch. I accepted his apology and told him I was moving on. No point in staying mad at him, right? "It's fine," I said again.

Finally, I ran into Hailey, and she jumped on me and hugged me hard for saying yes to the scary movie. "It's fine," I found myself saying for the third time this morning. It seemed I was making people happy all over the place, which should have been great. There was only one problem: It didn't really feel that great. It didn't even feel fine.

Now I would be stuck seeing a movie I didn't want to see, interviewing someone at a really inconvenient time, and having lunch with someone who'd annoyed the heck out of me just yesterday. It made me flash back to the Know-It-All letter Mr. Trigg had forwarded to me just hours ago. There was even more to it than I'd first realized, something about spending your time in a way that makes you happy. I'd just need to mull it over some more.

★   ★   ★

At lunch Hailey chattered on happily about the scary movie. I nodded and acted like I cared while watching the door for Michael's arrival. Bored, I picked at my organic chicken-curry wrap and made a mental tally of the homework assignments I'd received so far today. Then I spotted Michael.

He got his lunch and, with his tray held aloft, crossed the room to join us. I felt a smile blooming on my face despite my best efforts to conceal it.

I couldn't help but be happy to see the guy, even though I was annoyed at him.

Hailey cocked her head and looked at me. "Oh! Michael's coming up behind me, isn't he?" she said.

"What?" I asked, looking back at her.

Hailey grinned. "I can tell! You've got your special lovey-dovey face on!"

And, of course, Michael plopped his tray down right after she spoke, just verifying everything she'd said. *Psychic Friend Drives Girl Batty.*

"Guess who I'm meeting after this?" he said, by way of greeting.

I shrugged, acting disinterested.

"Uh-oh! Are you still annoyed at me for yesterday even though you said you weren't?" he teased.

"Maybe. A little," I said. I didn't want to play games, but I did feel I'd glossed over it a bit quickly this morning.

Michael suddenly dropped to his knees with his hands folded, in begging posture. "Please, please, forgive me, Sam Martone, for being an idiot and a rude person. I apologize. I'm begging your forgiveness!"

I covered my face with my hands in mortification as kids at other tables turned to stare at the spectacle he was making.

"Get up! Please! Get up!" I said through my hands. My face was burning with embarrassment.

"Only if you really and truly accept my apology!" he demanded from the floor.

"Fine! Just get up!" I peeked through my fingers. I could see Hailey laughing and clapping with joy.

"Nope! You have to say it. Say you forgive me!"

"Okay! I forgive you!" I cried, and he got up.

"See how easy that was?" he said, settling into his seat and beginning to eat.

"You are so embarrassing!" I said, my blush starting to subside.

"That was awesome!" Hailey giggled. "People thought you were proposing!"

"Oh, please!" I protested, mortified. *Note to self: Fire Hailey as best friend later.*

Michael just grinned and kept shoveling food

into his mouth, so I decided to change the subject. "So who are you meeting after this?" I asked.

"John Scott!" he replied, taking a bite out of his roll and chewing.

"Oh, interesting. I'm meeting him for lunch on Friday and Anthony at five that day."

"I think I'd better meet with Anthony again, too," he said between bites.

"I'm going to do the research tomorrow. By the way, I'll look in the *Cherry Valley Voice* for you while I'm there, to see if there's anything you need on John. So you'll be meeting them cold, and I'll be meeting them maybe prejudiced or maybe with an agenda, depending on what I find in my research. That should be fair, anyway," I said.

He nodded. "Then let's set up our Buddybook poll for the weekend. Just a simple 'Who's Your Candidate?' poll. No posting, no saying why. Just 'Who gets your vote?' Okay?"

I nodded my agreement. "Don't tell me anything before I meet with these guys," I said. "I don't want your observations to cloud my opinion.

I want to think for myself," I said.

"Don't you always?" mused Michael.

"Yes!" Hailey nodded emphatically.

"Hey! No comments from the peanut gallery!" I said. It was something my mom always said; I think it's from a TV show when she was little.

"Okay, so lunch Monday, then, to compare notes?" suggested Michael. It seemed so far off.

"Sure," I agreed. "If we don't see each other before then . . ."

"Yeah, like at the movies Friday night!" said Hailey.

I stared daggers at her.

"Oh, what are you going to see?" asked Michael as he gathered up his stuff to leave for the interview.

Hailey shrugged casually. "That new scary action movie everyone's talking about."

"What? Are you kidding me? That's supposed to be awesome! Can I come?"

Now I truly hated Hailey.

"You'll have to ask the boss," said Hailey, raising her eyebrows and gesturing toward me.

"Is it okay if I come?" he asked.

It's fine, I almost said. But it wasn't. I knew Hailey would be okay with it, but she sometimes gets her feelings hurt if I talk about Michael too much or if I try to involve him. We had been planning this for a long time. I needed to speak up or risk doing something against my own best interests again.

"You know what? I'd love to see it with you and I don't want to be mean, but we're doing a girls' night with Jenna and Kristen that night—dinner and a movie. Maybe I can see it with you at another time"—I winced at the thought of seeing it twice—"but we just can't sit with you Friday. I'm sorry. For real," I said. My stomach was in knots, dreading his reply by the time I'd finished talking.

But Michael nodded. "I totally get it. You girls go, and I might get a bunch of guys together if I get organized. Maybe if we're all there, we could grab some ice cream after or something. Unless that would that be in violation of girls' night?" He grinned his adorable grin and his eyes twinkled.

"That would be fine," I said calmly.

Hailey was still smiling.

"Okay, catch you later," he said as he took his tray and left.

"Good luck!" I called after him.

"See you Friday night!" called Hailey.

And then I did what any girl would have done to her BFF in the same situation.

I kicked her.

Chapter 5

JOURNALIST MAKES RIGHT CHOICE

★ ★ ★

At the library on Thursday, I searched the digital archive of the back issues of the *Voice* from the past two years. Anthony and John would have been mentioned only while they were students here, and since they were eighth graders now, it meant I didn't have to go back years and sift through tons of articles to find info about them.

I really love research, and I'm pretty good at it, I have to say. While I longed for the kind of well-researched files that Mr. Trigg had described the other day, I didn't mind putting together my own. Here's what I found about each of the candidates:

- John Scott writes a lot of letters to the editor.
- Anthony Wright has won three major

chess competitions, one of them statewide, and he is a nationally ranked competitor.
- John Scott is on the debate team and is the founder and president of the Young Republicans club at school.
- Anthony is in the Model UN club.
- John's older brother went here and graduated the year before I got here.
- Anthony's mom is a nutritionist and spoke at a PTA meeting.

None of this was exactly earth-shattering, and I was a little disappointed. I'd hoped to find some juicy tidbit to run in our article—what, I don't know. It wasn't like the school newspaper printed the week's arrests or anything (not that they'd been arrested!). I guess I just have this fantasy that our school election will be as jazzy as the real ones I read about all the time, but the truth is, it isn't that jazzy.

The candidates are kids. They've never really done anything else that we could dig up info about (like held a job in a public corporation or filed taxes), and they haven't been working toward this office for years like real candidates. All we'll know of them is what they'll tell us about themselves. It's all going to be "the message," as the blogs call it.

I stared into space at the computer terminal and drummed my fingers on the table, wishing a bombshell would materialize in print. When it didn't, I sighed and logged off. Maybe I'd find something in my "person-on-the-street" interviews. I made a list of questions in my notebook; then I set out to do a few interviews now, just to appease my hunger for information.

The first person I nabbed at my post outside the newsroom was a sixth grader named Sara Freund, a girl in sports clothes who didn't look like she was in a rush. I asked if she'd be willing to talk on the record for attribution in the school newspaper (in other words, I'd use her name), and she agreed.

"Okay," I began, pen poised above the paper in my notebook. "What do you think of John Scott, candidate for school president?"

"Um, I don't know him," she said. "Sorry."

"That's okay." I nodded supportively. "Have you heard of him?"

"Is he the guy who's in that band that played at the talent show?" she asked, a perplexed look on her face as she tried to place him.

"No . . . that was Scott Johnson. Close!"

"Yeah, so I've never heard of John Scott."

"Okay. How about Anthony Wright?" I asked in a chipper voice.

She shook her head again. "Sorry. I don't know him, either," she admitted. "I guess I'm a lousy interview."

"That's fine. I'm just getting started. Maybe you've just highlighted an interesting point. Maybe they're not that well known to underclassmen. Are you interested in the election?" I asked.

"Well, I just got to Cherry Valley, so . . . I don't really know what the issues are."

"Okay, so the underclassmen need to be made aware of the issues," I said, writing swiftly.

"Or maybe just I do?" she asked.

I stopped writing. "Oh. Good point. Well, I'd

better talk to some more sixth graders," I said. "Thanks."

The next kid I stopped was a sixth-grade boy named Henry Graham. He agreed to talk on the record, too, but hadn't heard of either of the candidates and also didn't know the issues.

"That's great! Thank you!" I said, happy to be building a theme. (***Sixth Graders Apathetic About Election!*** ran the headline in my mind.) He walked away with a puzzled look on his face but I was pleased.

A seventh grader named Tim Howard stopped. He said I could quote him but not use his name. He knew Anthony Wright and said he was nice if a bit nerdy, but most of all, he was stunned that Anthony would run for office. "Anthony? The *chess* guy? For school *president*?" he kept repeating incredulously. It was pretty annoying.

I was relieved to see Kristen and her friend Pam coming toward me in the hall. "Pam! Kristen!" I waved them over. "I need some quotes about the candidates, for the paper. Can I use your names?"

"Sure," they agreed.

Pam told me John Scott was hilarious and so fun in her language arts class. She said Anthony Wright was "quiet, but nice."

Kristen agreed John was fun and charming, and she said she didn't know Anthony well enough to comment.

Okay, so the candidates are known to most upperclassmen, so far, I theorized.

I grabbed a few more kids, all ages, until it was time to go to my next class. And they were all the same: The sixth graders had never heard of either of them, didn't know anything about the election process or the issues. The seventh graders knew one or the other (most knew John Scott, and those who knew Anthony were surprised he was running), had a few vague ideas of the process, and knew one or two things that the school president might be interested in working on. Finally, most of the eighth graders knew both, loved John Scott, were surprised at the idea of Anthony Wright running for school president, and had a pretty decent grip on the election process and the issues facing the school (food, sports team fees, music and art programming being cut, needing tutoring or extra help for hard classes). I was pretty impressed with the eighth graders, actually.

Obviously, I had more interviews to do, and Michael would need to do some too to make sure I tried being completely fair when I asked my questions. I mean, I try hard to be neutral (it's not like I say, "And can you *believe* that Anthony Wright is running?"), but you have to be so careful in the way you ask questions, so I just need to remember that and address it.

The article was starting to take shape in my mind—the intro at least. Uninterested sixth graders, voting solely on what the candidates tell them. Eighth graders clearly preferring one candidate over the other, on reputation alone. And seventh graders undecided, with some knowing a candidate personally and some not. I couldn't wait for my interviews to pull this whole thing together in my mind and then on paper.

★　★　★

At lunch Friday I secured two seats in a quiet area, leaving my messenger bag and jean jacket on them to save them while I got my lunch. I went to get a sandwich and look for John Scott. He was about ten minutes late, which actually was a little annoying but worked out to my advantage since I'd finished eating and could concentrate on the interview while he ate. I did make a little note of it though; lateness can reveal a person's character in many ways.

When John arrived, he got his food and joined me at the table, with a brief apology about his tardiness.

"Samantha Martone!" he began with a friendly grin. "It's an honor to be interviewed by a journalist of your caliber."

"I'm sorry, what?"

"I can't believe you're interviewing me!" John said. "After reading your articles in every issue—the Pay to Play article was awesome, the school lunch article intense, and I loved the coverage last year on the new curriculum—I always feel I have my finger on the pulse. You're always on the front page and always hitting the most important issues. I could take my campaign plan straight from your articles in the *Cherry Valley Voice*! And the writing! So good." He shook his head admiringly.

"Wow. Thanks! I'm flattered," I said, a tiny blush reddening my cheeks. "I can't believe you read all that."

"Well . . ." John stopped to find a fresh napkin on the table and spied my notebook. "Wait. You use a notebook?"

Surprised, I looked down at my trusty brown notebook. "Uhhh . . . yeah?" What was wrong with it? It looked okay to me.

John shook his head sadly. "Samantha—one of the first things I will do if elected school president is make certain everyone on the *Cherry Valley Voice* staff receives state-of-the-art iPads. How can you do your best work if you're not using the best equipment?"

"Really? Wow. That would be awesome!" I said excitedly, thinking how cool it would be to tote around an iPad for my articles. It would make things so much easier: online research, editing drafts, sharing with Michael. Not that

I'd ever had many problems with my notebook before, but still.

I glanced at my list of questions about John's background and qualifications; then I decided to just go with the flow of the conversation. "So, what else would you do if you were elected school president?" I asked, uncapping my pen and poising it above the page.

John brightened, and he pushed his tray away and folded his hands earnestly on the table in front of him. "Well, first of all, extra-long lunch breaks . . . How can the teachers expect us to work if we're not properly rested? Next, less homework—it's a proven fact that stress is not healthy for *anyone*, and homework adds a lot of stress to a student's life. Third, more extra-curriculars. Like, why don't we have film class? That would be so cool. Fourth . . ."

John outlined about ten great ideas while I nodded along and scribbled quickly to get it all down on paper before our hour was up. I could see what John envisioned for our school, and it was exciting. School life would be much better with John Scott at the helm! Plus, his delivery was amazing—I was objective enough to see that, though I actually had to fight myself from becoming totally charmed by his friendly voice, his sense of humor, and his enthusiasm.

After he outlined his plan, I asked him a couple of questions about his background, including about his family.

John was ready for this, too. "Well, I'm from a very small, tight-knit family: just me, my parents, and my older brother. We spend a lot of time together, and my brother and I are kind of our parents' life: They never miss a game or a debate; they quiz us at the table on current events; they drive us to all our lessons and stuff. We get along very well," he said proudly. "Also, I don't know if you've heard this story, but it's something I'm very proud of. I saved a little girl from drowning at the town lake two summers ago . . ."

"So, that *was* you!"

He nodded proudly. "Yup." He filled me in on the details, which were exciting but basically amounted to him yanking her out of the water before anything really bad happened and calling

911 on his brother's phone. Still, he did think fast. He finished the story by patting his heart. "Anna and I are still very close."

"Wow. What a wonderful story!" I said. "And your qualifications?"

John nodded, like he had practiced for this question. "I've written a great deal to the *Voice* about my positions on things in the news here. If you scroll through the back issues, you'll see I've basically gone on record on all of the major things facing this school. I'm on the debate team, so I know how to stand up for what I believe in and I'm good at public speaking, which is an important part of being school president. I'm very engaged in politics in the larger world and always follow elections closely." He held his hands out to me like he was offering me something and grinned. "I'm an open book! No secrets!" he said.

I chuckled. "I wasn't worried you'd have secrets," I said. "This all pretty much lines up with what I already knew about you," I said.

"Oho! What did you already know?" he asked teasingly.

"Just good stuff, I swear," I said, smiling down into my notebook. He was very charming.

"I sure hope so!" He laughed. "Otherwise I'll have to work hard for your vote!"

"Oh, I wouldn't worry too much about that," I said, but then I stopped, remembering I was supposed to be objective.

"Maybe you'd like to be my running mate, then," he said, a twinkle in his eye.

"Wait, what?"

"Do you want to?"

I was confused. "Do I want to be your *running mate*?"

He nodded.

I was flustered, like he'd suddenly asked me out on a date. I didn't know what to say. Me? Vice president of the school? It was a thrill to even consider it. Especially because John would probably win. I was flustered. "Uh, well . . . I've never really considered running for anything before. This is a little, uh, spontaneous. Are you serious?" I really didn't know what to say. I was confused, surprised, caught off guard. Like, had he seriously just asked me to be his running mate? It was a little weird but also a little flattering. More than a little flattering.

"I am very serious. Look, just consider it, okay?" he said generously. "I just know I need a female running mate, someone with a good name, a good reputation, cute, you know, to help me win. The whole package. And you're it!"

I scrunched up my eyebrows, confused. "Thanks?" I said, unsure but still flattered (he called me cute, after all!).

He looked at his watch. "I'd better let you go," he said, standing. We still had ten minutes before our next class, which was kind of a lot. I didn't really have anywhere to go, since my next class was literally two doors from the lunchroom. I suddenly had the sense that he'd just run this whole interview, and it was a weird feeling; now he was dismissing me.

"Uh . . . okay?" I scanned my notebook to see if I had any more questions, maybe a tough one. There were a couple, but they seemed a little harsh and nosy suddenly, especially after his complimentary invitation, so I snapped the book shut and stuck my hand out to shake his. "A pleasure doing business with you," I said formally.

"Likewise," he said, shaking my hand. "Let me know what you decide. And if you could . . . would you please let me know by tonight?"

That was another surprise. I felt a little off-kilter. "Tonight? Um, sure. Why so soon? The election isn't for another two weeks."

John shrugged and smiled his big megawatt grin again. "Gotta get on the campaign trail!"

"Right." I nodded. "Of course."

"Thanks, Samantha, for your time. Looking forward to seeing the piece when it comes out," he said.

"Just don't write a letter to the editor complaining about it!" I joked.

He gasped in mock horror. "Me? Would I do such a thing? Anyway, I know it will be a great and beautifully written piece!" he said.

"Bye!" I found myself smiling as he walked away.

I sat back down and breathed a sigh. His charm and energy were almost tiring. And the invitation to run with him? That was insane! But the more I thought about it, the more my stomach got kind of a funny happy feeling about it. I couldn't wait to discuss it with Hailey ASAP.

I scanned the room for her but instead spied Mr. Trigg across the lunchroom with a yogurt and a spoon, looking for a place to sit. Excited, I jumped up. "Mr. Trigg!" I called, and he looked my way. "Over here!" I cried, and he nodded and smiled and headed over to join me.

"Ms. Martone!" he said happily as he sat in John's recently vacated seat. "How lovely. One never gets over that preteen horror in cafeterias of not knowing where to sit."

I smiled. "I know. Even when your best friends are around, it can be tricky," I agreed.

"How was your lunch?" he asked.

"Great!" I said enthusiastically, and I filled him in on my interview with John Scott.

"Wonderful!" he said between bites of yogurt. "Sounds like a lovely chap!"

I nodded. "And you'll never guess what, Mr. Trigg. He asked me to join him as his running mate!"

Mr. Trigg put his yogurt down and his face broke into a huge smile. "Why, Samantha, you'd be splendid at that! Just terrific. You're so good with the faculty and administration. I can see it now! Of course, we'll miss you terribly, but you'd visit, right?"

I was confused. "Wait, what do you mean you'd miss me? I'll be right here still."

"No, but at the paper. We'd miss your writing and being a part of it all. You contribute such value to each edition."

"Why wouldn't I be at the paper anymore?" I asked.

"Well, you can't serve in the student government *and* cover it for the paper. Besides the issue of time management, it's a conflict of interest that we don't allow. So you'd have to choose. I completely understand your interest in student politics . . ."

"Wait, I couldn't write at all?" I asked again,

incredulous. How could I ever give up writing for the *Voice*?

Mr. Trigg thought for a minute. "I suppose you could continue with you-know-what." He raised his eyebrows to see if I understood.

I nodded at him, knowing he meant Dear Know-It-All.

"And perhaps, Ms. Martone, I could have you cover a sport . . . but everything else, I'm afraid"—he sighed heavily and shrugged—"off-limits."

I stared into the middle distance, thinking hard. "Oh," I said finally.

"Sorry," he said. "I thought you knew."

I shook my head. I couldn't give up the paper. No way. It was my favorite thing in the world, the thing I most enjoyed spending time on. It made me . . . me.

"Okay," I said. "Then I won't do it."

"Ms. Martone, at least give it a little thought! You've certainly put in a lot of time at the paper. Maybe you're ready for a change."

I shook my head, my campaign over before it had even begun. "No. No, I couldn't do that."

"Well then, welcome back, Ms. Martone!" joked Mr. Trigg, and I smiled back at him.

"Glad to be aboard," I joked back.

"Glad to have you!"

Journalist Makes Right Choice.

Chapter 6

UNDERDOG IMPRESSES STAR REPORTER

★   ★   ★

I caught up with Hailey by phone when I went home to change. I called her to say I might be a few minutes late to Slices but that she should order me two plain slices and a Coke and I'd be along as soon as I could. "And guess what?" I asked.

"What?"

"I almost ran for vice president of the school today!"

"Whaaaat?"

I explained it all quickly, and Hailey laughed. "I just lost the best job in the world!" she moaned.

"You? How?"

"Best friend of a powerful government official:

all of the perks, none of the headaches! I would've been great at that. Thanks a lot, Martone!"

"John Scott really is something, though. Boy, oh boy!" I said.

"Wait, does Mikey have a little competition here?" teased Hailey.

"No, no. Not like that. He's just . . . exciting. He'll make a great school president. That's all."

"Really?" singsonged Hailey.

"Really," I said firmly, but I had to smile.

"Okay, good. Because I'd hate to see Mikey's heart broken," she said.

"Please! As if!" I protested, but I did hope she was right, of course.

Giggling, we hung up, and I dashed off an e-mail to John Scott, declining his generous offer. I pushed send with a heavy heart, but I knew it was the right thing to do. Then I hurried to primp a little, in case we did run into Michael and go for ice cream after the movie. I put on a cute pink turtleneck sweater, earrings, my faded jeans with a pretty belt, and even a little bit of clear lip gloss. Then I got my things together for my interview at the Java Stop with Anthony Wright, grabbed my messenger bag and notebook, and headed out. As I walked over there, I thought about Anthony and his nerdy image. I felt bad for the guy; he was such an underdog. It must feel awful to run against someone and kind of know you're going to lose.

Or at least that's what I thought before the interview.

Afterward, it was all I could do to stop myself from quitting the paper and begging to be his running mate.

At the Java Stop, Anthony was already waiting for me.

"I'm so sorry!" I said, rushing to his table and struggling to see my watch under my shirt cuff. "Am I late?"

Anthony stood in a display of old-fashioned good manners as I seated myself; he even tried to pull out my chair for me. As he did so, he laughed a shy laugh. "No, you're not late. I'm compulsively early. Sorry. It comes from being the youngest of five in a family with a single mother. If I'm not ready to go when everyone else is, they'll leave me behind!"

It was sweet the way he said it, not like he felt sorry for himself or anything, just plain and factual. I was charmed again by his deep, warm voice, and was suddenly excited about this interview. We compared notes for a few minutes on being raised by single moms before getting down to business.

"So, in the interest of time, I should start asking you some of my questions," I said, pulling out my notebook and pen. "I'm sorry, but I have to leave by quarter of six."

"No, please. You're so nice to fit me in. I really appreciate it. We all pitch in after school with baby-sitting and activities before my mom gets home from work, so it's always crazy schedule-wise. I wish I could join a lot more things at school, but as it is, I've had to choose just the ones that I really like the most. Anyway, I appreciate that you are taking the time to meet with me. . . . It's hard for me to get my message out. I'm not a natural public speaker like John Scott is, and I'm not as well known, so this will really help." He smiled at me, his teeth strong and bright, his smile genuine and a little shy. It was the first time I'd really seen his smile and he had a great one—contagious.

I smiled back. "Okay, first of all, tell me about the chess. I know it doesn't really apply, but it's all I read about you!" I joked.

But Anthony grew serious. "Actually, it kind of does apply. For one thing, I want to talk about how I got into it. I started playing at an after-school care program I went to starting in first grade. It was a state-funded program, and it really was so important to me. It gave me and a couple of my brothers somewhere to go after school while our mom got her graduate degree in nursing, and it got each of us into an activity that we love and still stick with. One of my brothers plays basketball, another is a math champion, and I do chess."

I nodded for him to go on as my pen flew across the page, taking notes.

"The program lost its funding after our first two years, and for us, it was kind of okay since we were older and my mom was done with school.

But I look back on lots of kids who had no other options, and I see what a shame it is that the program folded. I'd love to see something like that start at Cherry Valley. I have some ideas on how to fund it, too."

"That would be great," I agreed.

He cleared his throat and continued. "Okay, so second of all, chess is great strategic training. It teaches you to plan ahead, think of your next move, be patient. You can't play chess with a hot head. I've learned to control my temper, manage my emotions, take things in stride, think on the go. All good."

I raised my eyebrows. "I've never thought of that side of it before."

He nodded. "It's a great game. Then there's the competition aspect. For me, it has been really fun to see how far I can go with this. Competing has meant organizing my schedule to accommodate the tournaments and the travel, learning to get my work done efficiently and manage my time effectively. It has also given me a lot of independence and self-reliance, since I have to get my own rides to the games, make my own money for the entry fees, stuff like that. And I pack my own lunch!" He laughed.

"Does your family like that you do it?"

Anthony looked down shyly. "They love it because I love it, and they like seeing me happy. They do come when they can."

"Cool," I said, impressed. "You've certainly done well at it. County champion, statewide runner up. Captain of the school chess team your first year."

He shrugged modestly. "I enjoy it. Chess has been good to me."

"And what else would you have in mind for the school?"

Anthony began outlining his goals, his long, tapered fingers gesturing beautifully as he spoke. He came so alive talking about his goals and plans for Cherry Valley Middle School, modest though they were, that I stopped seeing his nerdiness and almost saw him as an adult. He sure talked like one—in a good way. I could hardly write fast enough to keep up. His ideas weren't flashy like John's idea to make lunch longer or have less homework, but they were much more thoughtful. Anthony was very cost-conscious and very academically oriented. He had a good sense of the school's mission and goals, as well as what its challenges were. He said he saw himself as an advocate for the students and a liaison between the kids and the adults in the community. He had done a ton of research on funding and budgets and felt he knew what was doable and what wasn't. Hmm. *Underdog Impresses Star Reporter.*

One of his good ideas was having high school students supervise after-school care for the middle schoolers, either proctoring study halls or sharing skills. It could be a for-credit course they designed and committed to for the semester, or something they did to satisfy their volunteering requirements for graduation. The high schoolers would act as mentors for the middle schoolers. Anthony had even contacted a big national foundation and learned it was just the kind of innovation they liked to fund in public schools. He didn't have a guarantee yet, but his contact there was interested. So he'd met with the principal and the guidance counselors at the high school and they were raring to go on the program.

Another idea he had was homework buddies. Again, free, but something that allowed students who were strong in one area to be paired with kids who needed help in other areas, kind of like me and Hailey.

He also wanted to start something called "working lunches" where authors would visit over lunch and speak to students about their work, and maybe a visiting scientist or mathematician program as well, to get kids thinking about the future and how they could apply their skills in different careers. I thought about Mr. Trigg already factoring in college recommendations. It was a really good idea.

He'd also looked into securing a grant from a company that taught kids how to grow and prepare some of their own lunch food, as our school chef had hoped they one day could, maybe even raising chickens in the side yard of the school. Chickens at school might be a long shot, but the idea was definitely cool.

At a certain point, I smiled and he caught me. "What? What's so funny?" he asked, already grinning in anticipation of the joke.

I sighed and shook my head. "Just that John Scott is talking about less homework and longer lunch periods, iPads and gourmet food, and you're talking about whether we can afford an after-school program for kids who really need it. It's a big contrast."

Anthony looked a little dejected. "I know. My stuff is not as appealing."

I titled my head and looked at him. "Don't get down on yourself. You're realistic, and you've done a ton of legwork. John's . . . a politician." I shrugged. "I think your ideas are amazing!"

He looked up and squared his shoulders. "I may not be the most exciting candidate, but I'm the right one. John Scott has to realize how overbudget the school is already. There's barely enough money in the budget to buy new pencil sharpeners, much less iPads! And longer lunch periods and less homework? Doesn't he realize the school has to conform to a set curriculum that mandates how long periods can be and things like that?" He scoffed in disgust. "I wish I could get my message out—jazz it up. Make it sound fun and cool."

I tapped my pen against my teeth and thought for a second while he took a sip of his peppermint tea. If only Anthony could have a campaign manager. Someone stylish and focused on presentation, good at giving advice, someone who knew how to get the word out on Buddybook or Twitter . . .

"I've got it!" I cried. Anthony leaned close to hear my idea and then . . .

Poof!

A flash went off and nearly blinded us. I turned to see what it was and found Jeff Perry squatting near our table.

"Jeff!"

"Hey. Couldn't resist a shot of such a heated conversation. What could be so exciting that you two are mere inches apart? This could make quite an interesting photo of life on the campaign trail. Awfully cozy for a reporter and a candidate, aren't we?"

I scrunched my eyebrows. What the heck was he talking about? I looked at Anthony in confusion, and he seemed as perplexed as I was.

"What?" he asked Jeff.

Jeff shrugged. "A picture's worth a thousand words," he said, and then he walked away.

Anthony and I looked at each other. "What*ever*," I said, and rolled my eyes. "Listen, here's my idea, and then I've got to run. . . . Anthony, you've got to meet my sister, Allie." I filled him in, and he was eager to meet her.

"Why not? Let's do it!" he said.

We high-fived, and then I looked at my watch. "Darn it! I'm going to be late!" I said; then I clapped my hand over my mouth. "I'm sorry. I didn't mean to be rude. It's just that I wish we had more time!"

"Thanks," said Anthony with a smile. "Me too. You're easy to talk to."

"Anything else I should know about you before I go? Save any toddlers from drowning or anything?"

He laughed and shook his head. "I'm afraid not."

"Don't worry. I think that's probably a good thing!" I said. "Thanks. I'll get in touch about Allie ASAP."

"Thanks, Sam!"

★   ★   ★

I did end up being late for Slices. And the other three girls were halfway through their pizza when I arrived, breathless.

"I'm so sorry!" I cried, lunging into the booth to where Hailey had set my two slices and Coke.

But no one seemed perturbed by my lateness.

"First she says no to the cute boys; then she's late . . . !" joked Hailey.

"Sorry," I said guiltily. "Michael said he and some friends might, just *might* come, and if so they'll meet us after for ice cream. They probably won't make it, though. You know how boys are so disorganized." Then I thought of Anthony and, actually, Michael too, and I corrected myself. "Well, some of them are disorganized. Anyway, how much time do we have before we have to leave for the movie?"

Kristen looked at her watch. "Ten minutes."

"Phew," I said, and relaxed a little.

"Yeah, we know you wouldn't want to miss a minute of it," said Jenna, her eyes twinkling.

Hailey fluffed her hair and tossed her head. "Well, I sure wouldn't!"

We all laughed. "We know!" I said, taking a bite of the crispy, thin-crust pizza.

"So who were you interviewing?" asked Jenna, sipping at the dregs of her soda.

I swallowed hard and said, "Anthony Wright!"

"Oh yeah! How was he?" asked Kristen.

"Actually . . . I'm not supposed to say, because I'm an unbiased reporter." I took another bite of pizza and smiled.

"Come on! Just tell us objectively!" said Jenna.

I looked at them all point-blank as I chewed and then swallowed. "He was awesome." I took another bite.

"Whaaaat? Anthony Wright? Are you serious?" said Hailey incredulously. "How?"

At this rate I was never going to finish eating in time. "Let's just say this guy has seriously done his homework. He's not promising glamorous stuff, but he *is* realistic and has some really cool ideas that he's able to follow through on. I thought he was really, really good."

"Is he promising steam showers in the locker room like John Scott's going to get us?" asked Hailey.

"Yeah, or a new art studio with a glass wall to let the northern light in?" asked Jenna. "John's going to get us that, too."

"And a new gymnastics studio. I can't wait!" said Kristen.

"Wow," I said, starting to feel even more skeptical about John Scott. "That guy's got a lot more promises than Anthony Wright. But Anthony's are at least realistic. I think he could really win."

Hailey looked thoughtful. "Too bad he's so nerdy."

"Yeah," agreed Jenna. "He needs a makeover."

"Bingo!" I cried, pointing my greasy, wadded-up napkin at her. "My thoughts exactly. And who's just the person to do the job?" I asked them all.

"You?" said Jenna tentatively.

Kristen was stumped.

Hailey's eyes widened as she got it. "Allie!"

she breathed reverently. Hailey worships Allie. "O-M-G, Sammy, that is genius."

"What is Allie, like, the Makeover Queen?" asked Kristen.

"Mm-hmm," I said through a mouthful of pizza.

"You have no idea," said Hailey worshipfully.

I crunched on my crust and looked at my watch. "Should we head out?" I asked.

Everyone stood up and tossed their garbage; then we made our way over to the theater. Sure enough, who was in line but old Mikey himself. Hailey flashed a megawatt grin of happiness for me, and I smiled back. I caught Michael searching the crowd, and when he saw me, he stopped and grinned. "There you are!" he called. I waved. "See you in there!" He nodded. "Girls' night!" he replied, and he continued on to the ticket taker.

I smiled happily to myself and turned back to my friends, who were all grinning at me.

"*He might not come*," teased Hailey.

"Oh, shush, you!" I said happily.

Chapter 7

BEST FRIEND IS MORTIFIED, REFUSES TO BE COMFORTED

★ ★ ★

Opening night of a new scary movie is wild in our town. The show was sold out (thankfully Hailey had had her dad buy our tickets online in advance), and we were lucky to find four seats together. Of course, we were smushed up against the wall, but it was better than being scattered. I craned my head to search the theater and find Michael, finally locating the cute back of his head in the middle toward the front. He was with annoying Jeff Perry (rogue photographer!), his friend Frank Duane, and a couple of other guys I didn't recognize from behind.

Hailey sat first, against the wall, then Jenna, Kristen, and me. Jenna and Kristen volunteered to go get snacks, and Hailey and I held down the fort, talking across the two empty seats.

"So was Anthony up for meeting Allie?" she asked.

I nodded. "Yeah, definitely. Whatever it takes, he said."

Hailey nodded. "You think he'll ask you to be his VP?" she joked.

"Nah. He's so good, I don't even think he needs one! But maybe we should try to think up a few suggestions for him anyway." I thought about who could balance him out. "He could use a girl, someone with a good reputation, if not downright popular, someone sporty, maybe not as academic as him. Someone . . ."

Suddenly Hailey let out an ear-piercing scream.

"What?" I jumped out of my seat and stared at her. She was pointing at the wall where a centipede was wiggling toward the light fixture.

Now, everyone has their phobias, and I know they're not rational. I hate snakes (normal), Allie hates mice (totally average), my mom hates roaches (common), but Hailey has phobias about clowns and centipedes. A little odd, don't you think? Go figure.

"Hails, it's all right." I grabbed my notebook out of my bag and stood and tried to give it a whack, but I couldn't reach it.

"Sam! It's crawling toward me now!" shrieked Hailey, her knees pulled up in front of her as if it were coming at her from the floor. "Get it!"

I flailed spastically at the multilegged insect as it wiggled across the wall, and I could feel people turning to stare.

Heroic Battle: Girl vs. . . . Centipede?

"Sam! EEEK!" screeched Hailey as I tried to whack it and fell over like the spaz that I am. I stood up to see a dad in the row in front of us give it a good whack with a newspaper, and it fell, dead, onto the floor, where the dad picked it up with a napkin and smiled at us.

"Thanks," muttered Hailey weakly.

Just then, Jenna and Kristen returned with the snacks and asked what was going on, and the lights started to dim. They hustled into their seats and handed out the candy and popcorn. I was just starting to relax when a boy's voice from down to the left yelled, "Eek, Sam! A mouse! Get it!" in a perfect imitation of Hailey. The crowd erupted in laughter, and as I turned to smile at Hailey, I found her pushing past me out of the row, up the aisle, and out of the theater.

I watched her go and then turned to Jenna and handed her my snacks. "I'll be right back," I said, and I went after Hailey.

I found her outside the theater, crying and mopping her face with a napkin. I put my arms around her for a hug, but Hailey just stood there stiffly.

"Hails, it was a joke," I said.

"A joke? It was humiliating!" she cried. "I'm never going to the movies again!"

"Oh, Hailey," I said lamely.

"Go back in. You don't need to stay here with me. I'll just call my mom to come get me," she said, sniffling. *Best Friend Is Mortified, Refuses to Be Comforted.*

"No way. I'm not leaving you."

"But the movie . . ."

"Hailey, really? I think I'll live."

"All your stuff is in there," she said lamely, not trying that hard to get rid of me. I think my staying was actually making her feel a tad better.

I shrugged. "Jenna and Kristen will bring it out after. Want to play Angry Birds on the machine over there?"

She shrugged a yes, and we went over and began pumping the machine with whatever quarters we had in our pockets. When that ran out, we sat on a bench in the theater lobby. She seemed to have calmed down.

"Do you still want to go home?" I asked. "I'll go with you if you want."

"No, you can't miss your ice-cream date," she teased.

Now it was me who shrugged. "Whatever," I said. "It's girls' night."

"Thanks," she said. "I just don't want to be sitting here like a loser when the movie gets out, is all. Maybe we could wait for them at the ice-cream place."

We were quiet for a minute.

"Sammy?" asked Hailey in a small voice.

I turned and looked at her. "What?"

Hailey looked down at her nails, what little she hadn't already bitten off. "Um, before the bug thing, you were talking about stuff." She sighed and looked up at the ceiling searchingly. "Like, about Anthony Wright?"

I shook my head. "I don't remember. Trauma causes memory loss."

She smiled wanly. "Like, about a running mate for him. You were describing what he needed. It . . . it sounded like . . ."

"You," I said at the exact same moment she said, "Me."

We laughed.

"What do you think?" she asked.

"About you running for vice president with Anthony?"

Hailey nodded.

"Would you want to?" I asked.

Hailey looked back at her nails again and nodded again. "Yeah," she admitted, looking up at me.

"Huh!" I said, and smacked my knee with my palm. I was surprised, and I couldn't hide it. I sat there and thought about it for a minute. I felt a little bittersweet about it because it would have been fun for me to run too, except for the newspaper part. But I could actually see Hailey doing it, the more I thought about it. She's a hard worker who likes to win; she's captain of the varsity soccer team again, and she knows how to lead and inspire people. She'd be a good cheerleader for him, too. And she did have lots of friends in parts of the school where Anthony really doesn't. "I think it's a great idea!" I said enthusiastically.

Hailey's head snapped up. "Really?" She grinned.

"Really," I said. "And then *I* get the best job in the world!"

We laughed, remembering Hailey's comment from earlier.

"I'll talk to him, then. He might not want me," Hailey said.

"Yeah, he'll probably need a Centipede Warrior, and you are just not that person," I teased.

Hailey punched me hard in the arm.

"Ow!" I cried, rubbing my arm. "Come on. Let's go back in. We can't sit here for another hour and a half till those guys all come out."

"I guess." But Hailey's eyes grew wide and frightened. "Do you think there are more centipedes in there?"

"No," I said firmly. "And anyway, I'm here to protect you. I'll be like the Secret Service."

★   ★   ★

As soon as the credits rolled but before they turned on the lights, Hailey jumped up and whispered, "Come get me in the bathroom once everyone's gone," and she took off.

Great public confidence, I thought. *Oh boy.*

Outside the theater, Jenna, Kristen, and I waited for Michael and his gang. When they came out, they were all jostling around and joking. Action movies get boys so jazzed up, like they want to go out and save the planet too. It's kind of how I feel after I see a movie with ballet in it—like I want to go pirouette across the mall.

Anyway, we made a plan to head to Scoops for

ice cream, and I said I'd be right along. Michael tried to hang back and wait for me, but I whispered that I had to get Hailey, so he rejoined the group.

In the bathroom I spotted Hailey's sneakers under a stall and called her out; then we headed over to Scoop.

"I'm mortified again," said Hailey.

"Get over it," I said sternly. "If you're going to run for office, you'd better have some thick skin."

"Really?" asked Hailey.

I nodded.

"Oh," she said. "Okay."

At Scoop, Hailey and I separated, and I sat in a conveniently empty seat next to Michael. We talked about the movie briefly, but as usual, we really wanted to talk about the paper, so we got right to it.

"I met with John Scott *and* Anthony Wright today, both," I said, taking a bite of my coffee ice cream with hot fudge sauce.

"And?" said Michael.

"Wait, you've met them both, right?" I asked.

He nodded, his eyes twinkling. "What did you think?"

I chewed the fudge thoughtfully and then said, "Loved Wright, surprisingly, but he takes a little time to get to know. Scott is the obvious choice, but he's more style over substance."

"Lots of pie-in-the-sky ideas, right?" said Michael, nodding.

I nodded back in agreement. "Like, how's he going to pull all that off?"

"I know. He was pretty flattering, though. He knew all about my win/loss record for pitching; he named a bunch of my articles for the paper . . ." Michael looked away shyly. "He even asked me to be his running mate."

"Wait, what? Me too! He asked me to be his running mate too!"

Michael whipped his head back and stared at me in shock; then we both began to laugh hard.

"O-M-G, is that a campaign tactic?" I said, still laughing incredulously.

"Seriously? I can't believe it. He told me I was the ideal choice because I'm athletic, I'm a good writer, so I could 'craft out strategy,' and stuff like that." Michael was shaking his head in dismay.

I said, "He told me that because I'm a girl and I'm cute, I'd be a good match for him."

Michael looked at me, and his face was kind of angry. "Are you serious? That is so out of line." He was mad, and it took me aback a little.

"Well, I thought it was kind of flattering." I laughed.

"Now I hate that guy," said Michael.

"Whoa! Objectivity? Impartial press?"

"Not anymore," said Michael.

"Wait, are you mad that he asked us both and flattered us both, or . . . is it something else?" I knew I was kind of fishing, but I had to!

"Both," said Michael. "That guy has a lot of nerve."

"Yeah, I think that's the point. And Anthony doesn't."

Michael was thoughtful then. "I wouldn't say that. I think Anthony actually has a ton of nerve. The way he stood up to that mugger . . . Did you read that article? And the time he—"

"Wait, mugger? Article? Where?"

Michael looked at me. "He didn't tell you that story? I guess I found it when I Googled him, and then I asked him about it. He didn't really want to talk about it, but he was a hero, pretty much. A guy tried to steal his mom's purse in the park near their house, and Anthony knocked him down and pinned him while his mom called the cops. Pretty major stuff."

"Wow! I had no idea! I tried Googling those guys, but there was so much to wade through." I remembered wishing for the old profiles Mr. Trigg had talked about. "That's pretty funny, because John Scott told me his 'saving the toddler' story immediately, but when I asked Anthony if he had a hero story I could write about, he said no. Pretty modest, right?"

Michael nodded. "He's impressive, that guy."

"Yeah, it's like he's the right one, but it's such a popularity contest that it'll be John Scott the professional politician who wins. Just like in real life," I said mournfully.

"I don't know. We have a chance to help him

out. We could do a great profile in the paper on Anthony."

"We'd have to do one on John, too, that's as good."

Michael was nodding. "We will. It's just that the stories and plans will speak for themselves."

I nodded. "Also, I'm getting my sister to spruce Anthony up a little. And I think Hailey should be his running mate."

Michael laughed. "Impartial, huh? Sounds like you're his campaign manager!"

"Well, it sounded like you were John Scott's VP there for a minute!"

Michael shook his head. "I wouldn't want to leave the paper for anything. I love spending—" He stopped short and gave me a surprised, kind of guilty look. "I mean, I love it."

I smiled a small smile, hoping he'd been about to say what I wanted to hear. "How did you know the thing about the conflict of interest? I had to have Trigg tell me. It was so embarrassing that I didn't know you couldn't do both."

"Um, Pasty? Hello? Common sense?"

"Oh, shut up!" I said, giving him a playful whack.

"Hey, what are you two lovebirds—I mean writing partners—up to over here?" said Hailey. She'd come around the table and joined us.

"Eek! It's Hailey!" teased Michael.

Hailey's face fell.

"Um, touchy subject. Not funny," I said.

Michael looked at her in surprise. "I'm sorry. Were you upset about that? For real?"

Hailey shrugged. "It was mortifying!"

"It was funny! Everyone loved it!"

"Yeah, but that guy down in front, making fun of me? That was the worst. I'll never live it down!" she wailed.

"But Greg wasn't teasing you to be mean. I think he was doing it to get your attention."

"Greg who?" said Hailey, perplexed.

"Gregory Toms," said Michael. "I thought you knew it was him."

"Why would Gregory Toms want my attention?" asked Hailey. Greg is one of the best-looking guys in our grade and superpopular.

Michael knocked on Hailey's head. "Hello? Anyone home? He probably likes you!"

Hailey blushed and smiled a shy smile that she tried to hide. "So he teased me because he likes me?"

"Yeah. Why do you think I always call Sam Pasty?" said Michael with a mischievous grin.

We all laughed like it was a joke, but inside I prayed it was true.

"Look, Hails, everyone knows how awesome you are. You're funny, cute, superathletic Hailey . . . ," I said.

". . . who we all now know is afraid of creepy-crawly things at the movies!" Michael concluded.

"And who we want to run for school VP with Anthony Wright!" I added.

Hailey smiled, and we all got chatting about it. Pretty soon it was time for us to head out for our pickup by Hailey's dad. Jenna and Kristen went first and were waiting for us outside Scoops as we said good-bye to the boys.

"Eek!" annoying Jeff Perry called after us as we left.

"Can it, Perry!" I called back. "I'm Secret Service, and that's my client you're making fun of!" And then Hailey and I laughed and laughed as we headed out.

Chapter 8

BEST FRIEND IRRELEVANT WHEN CAMPAIGN BUG BITES

★ ★ ★

As soon as I got home Friday night, I Googled Anthony and found the mugger article. It was an impressive story and gave a new dimension to him that people wouldn't normally know about. Never mind centipedes, this guy really was a warrior.

I organized a weekend training session between Allie and Anthony for Sunday afternoon. I decided to ask Hailey to come over at the same time, just to be around while Anthony was there and thinking about the campaign. She could introduce herself and maybe he'd just ask her to be his VP. I filled her in on all of his ideas and she thought they were awesome. She got roaming around the

Internet and had a list of foundations that might give grants to our school for programs as well as a short list of a few other cool ideas that sounded like they'd be interesting to Anthony.

I'd honestly never seen Hailey so jazzed for something before (something that didn't involve sneakers and sweating, anyway), and I was happy for her. I really, really hoped he'd pick her.

Allie had been eager to help, as I'd known she would be. There's nothing Allie loves more than a makeover, and since she hadn't really done one with a boy before, she was very excited about it. "I know his brother Jerome," she said. "He's a math genius. It's a known fact." Allie was impressed with these guys, and it's not that easy to impress her. (She's usually too busy tweeting or texting or Buddybooking or using some other media that hasn't even been named yet. She'll probably volunteer to be one of the guinea pigs when they figure out how to implant cell phones in our brains or something.) Anyway, she got online and started researching public speaking tips and how to make a good campaign speech. It was right up her alley. I bet she'll work in publicity when she grows up. She'd be darn good at it.

Anthony came over right after lunch on Sunday and was really charming with my mom, who I could tell was impressed by his manners and his maturity. Hailey showed up shortly after, and she and I sat in the kitchen and tried to eavesdrop on Allie and Anthony, who were working in my mom's office downstairs.

It was a little boring for me after a while, so I tried to make conversation. "So Gregory Toms, huh?" I said.

"Shh!" said Hailey, leaning out of her chair to listen in.

If Hailey didn't want to discuss the fact that Gregory Toms might like her, then something serious was going on. I went to get my notebook and start mapping out my profiles of the two candidates. It wasn't like I had anything else to do while she eavesdropped.

Best Friend Irrelevant When Campaign Bug Bites.

I lined up my person-on-the-street interview

quotes for each boy, as well as the articles I'd printed out from the school archives. Then I pulled out my transcripts from the interviews themselves.

I felt like I'd started the process being very *for* John Scott but ended up being for Anthony Wright instead. I knew a lot of people would feel the same way, if they could just get the opportunity to know Anthony better. I hoped Allie's strategy for him would include a Buddybook page where they could list all his achievements and link the article on the mugging.

Suddenly there was a shriek from my mom's office. Allie.

"What's wrong?" I called down the stairs.

"Samantha Martone! Come see this right now!" she yelled. Uh-oh. This didn't sound good.

Hailey and I bolted down the stairs two at a time and found them in front of a Buddybook page. They'd done a search for photos tagged with Anthony's name, and the photo filling the screen was the first to come up.

It was the photo Jeff Perry had taken of me and Anthony during our interview at the Java Stop on

Friday night. But it didn't look like an interview. It looked like a date. Our heads were so close together across the table, it looked like we were about to kiss, and I had an ecstatic look on my face and Anthony was smiling expectantly. It was actually a great shot, if only what it implied were true.

"Wow," I said.

"What the heck?" asked Hailey, looking at me and then Anthony in confusion.

Anthony laughed awkwardly. "Did they Photoshop that?" he asked in an embarrassed voice.

Allie just glared at me.

The caption under the photo said, "Is romance blooming on the campaign trail?"

I turned on my heel and stormed up the stairs to get the phone book.

I flipped to the Perrys' number and punched it into the phone so hard my fingertip hurt. Then I stood, tapping my foot impatiently until someone picked up.

"Hi, is Jeff there, please?" I said firmly.

"No, I'm sorry, he's not. May I take a message?" I think it was his mom.

I gave an annoyed sigh. "Yes. Please tell him Samantha Martone called and that I am not amused. He needs to take the photo down immediately."

"Okay. Will he know what this is in reference to?" asked his mom with a long-suffering sigh. She was pretty used to these calls, I'm sure. Jeff has a real thing for posting all kinds of trouble-causing photos online.

"Yes!" I snarled. "And thank you," I added in a nicer tone of voice, and I hung up the phone hard.

I stood in the kitchen and fumed for a minute. I could imagine how it felt to be a real politician, or a celebrity, when misleading pictures of you are printed all the time. I wouldn't be able to stand it. It was the injustice of it all that got to me.

Back downstairs, Allie had untagged the photo, so at least it wouldn't come up in a search. Then Hailey had instructed them to contact Buddybook to have the photo taken down in the meantime, which I didn't know you could do, and things were well on their way to being resolved. At least

Hailey had had a moment to shine in a crisis.

I stared at the photo. "That's right when I had the idea for Anthony to work with you, Allie," I said, thinking out loud.

"Yeah, right," said Allie, rolling her eyes.

"It's true, actually," agreed Anthony, and Allie softened.

"Well, at least you two look excited about it, so I guess I'm flattered," she said.

"Compliments come in the strangest ways," said Hailey knowingly. "Trust me."

I smiled.

Hailey swallowed hard, screwing up her courage, I could see; then she began asking Anthony pointed questions about his campaign platform. Allie joined in, and I left the three of them brainstorming, knowing that when I came back, there'd probably be a new VP candidate in town.

Upstairs, I had three IMs from Michael. The first one was kind of jokey. It said:

Saw the photo online of you and the next prez. Cozy.

The next one said:

It's all over Cherry Valley. Are you two a thing?

The third one said:

Sam, call me please.

I gulped and sat back in my desk chair. Michael calls me Sam only when he's serious or upset. This could be either. Or both. I drummed my fingers on my desk and tried to work up my courage to call Michael. Just then the phone rang, and I nearly jumped out of my skin. I ran into the upstairs hall to answer it, but Allie had already picked up. It was Jeff Perry. By the time she was done shouting at him, I didn't even need to speak to him. I just gingerly hung up the receiver and stood there with a small smile on my face. Luckily, Jeff Perry has an ego the size of an RV, so Allie's dressing-down wouldn't mortally wound him. He'd just take it in stride and look for the next opportunity to create chaos with a photo. And that's why he'll make a great paparazzo one day.

I lifted the receiver again and sighed in relief when I heard the dial tone. With shaky fingers and a dry mouth, I dialed Michael's number (yes, people, I know it by heart) and prayed he wouldn't answer. But he did. On the first ring.

"Hello?" he said.

"Michael?" I said.

"Sam," he said, sounding serious. "What's up?"

"Well . . . a lot? I guess?"

He sighed heavily. "Are you . . . ? I mean . . . Do you . . . ?"

"I don't like Anthony Wright like that," I blurted. "I am impressed by him, but it's not romantic. Jeff snapped that photo right at the end of the interview as I was pitching the idea of Allie helping him with his image. You can ask Anthony if you don't believe me."

There was a heavy silence at the other end of the phone.

"Hello?" I said.

"Yeah," said Michael dejectedly.

"What, are you bummed that I don't like him?" I said, laughing nervously. "What's up?"

"No, I just . . ."

"Not impartial enough for you?" I joked.

"Something like that," said Michael with a humorless laugh.

There was an awkward silence. I was dying to tell him I'd never like anyone else, but I was too scared and shy. Anyway, I wanted him to be the first to say it.

"Look . . ." "I . . ." We both spoke at the same time.

"So . . . um, are we all set for lunch on Monday?" I asked.

"Sure," said Michael in relief. "Yes. That sounds great."

"Okay then," I said. "Let's work on merging our rough drafts tomorrow, then we can divide it up for the final draft. We might need to meet after school on Wednesday just to finalize."

"Sounds good. Later, Paste," he said.

"Later, Mikey," I said, and smiled at the phone after I hung it up.

I sat at my computer and worked on my rough drafts for the interviews for about an hour; then I went to see what was up at campaign headquarters. The three of them had rolled up their sleeves and were working on Anthony's speech, and Allie was showing him how to stand and how to move as he delivered it and made his important points. It was pretty impressive that she just knows this stuff intuitively. I forgot she was my sister for a second and just stood watching her in her element. She was also counseling him on opening with a joke. She said it would be best if it wasn't scripted, but rather spontaneous. Something he could work in from the day's news or something that happened. Anthony seemed scared and frustrated by this idea, since he didn't want to leave anything to chance.

"I'm not very funny . . . ," he was saying.

"I am!" Hailey replied.

Then Allie saw me and said, "Sam, can you go make popcorn and get us some drinks or something? We're running out of steam down here."

"Please?" added Anthony.

"Please," said Allie, with an eye roll.

"Sure," I said, smiling at Anthony.

"The photo's down!" Hailey called after me.

"Phew!" I replied.

I had to admit that I felt a little left out. I mean, I was the one who'd set this whole thing up, and now I was fetching them snacks and stuff? It seemed a little lame, especially since I'd briefly considered running for VP myself just two days ago. *Easy come, easy go*, I thought. But were politics really my thing? I wasn't sure they were Hailey's, either, to be honest, but she seemed gung ho to try. They were certainly Anthony's thing. And John Scott's, just in a very different way. After reviewing my notes and working on the articles, I could see that John Scott was really in it for the glory of the office, and maybe not because he really wanted to do the work, while Anthony was the opposite.

The popcorn finished popping, and I took it out carefully and poured it into a bowl. I got a pitcher of iced tea out of the fridge and three glasses; then I did two trips down to the office to bring it to them.

"What are you up to now?" asked Hailey as they took a snack break.

"Working on my stories for the paper," I said.

Hailey sighed. "You're so lucky you get to do what you love for school."

"Well, you do too with soccer," I said.

"It's different, though. Soccer's not really 'school,'" said Hailey.

"In Ancient Greece and Rome, athletics were considered a huge and important part of life at school. The athletes were the leaders, and they even called their schools 'gymnasiums,'" offered Anthony.

"Hmm, that kind of sounds familiar from history class in fourth grade," I said.

"See, that's just the kind of comment that's going to *not* get you elected, Anthony," said Allie wryly. "Rein in the intellectualism and pump up the charm—remember, pal? Just until you get elected; then you can go all nerdy again, okay?" She smiled at him. I couldn't believe she could get away with the way she spoke to people, but they really listened to her.

Hailey was smiling at her adoringly, of course, and I wanted to puke.

"Can't wait to see the speech," I said to Anthony.

"It's this Friday!" he said with a nervous smile.

"Don't worry. We'll be ready," said Allie grimly.

"Go get 'em, tiger!" I said to her.

"Now back to the spontaneous joke," Allie said with a determined look on her face.

"Good luck," I whispered to the candidates as I tiptoed back out of the room.

Impartial Journalist Fired from Paper.

Oh boy.

Chapter 9

POLITICS TOO DIRTY, JOURNO RETIRES TO SPORTS PAGES

★ ★ ★

Lunch on Monday with Michael was good. We were uneasy at first, but once we started talking about our articles, we found an easy rhythm and all the weirdness of the weekend evaporated, thank goodness.

We went over the drafts of our articles to see how we could best merge them, and we made notations all over the pages. Then he took the one on John Scott and I took the one on Anthony Wright, and we laid out our plans for the rewrites. They were due Thursday morning, so we still had a little time. The paper would come out Friday. The results of our Buddybook poll showed John Scott leading about 75 percent to Anthony Wright's 25 percent. I was worried but working hard—maybe too hard—to keep my articles neutral.

The posters started appearing Tuesday:

JOHN SCOTT
the People's Choice
for
School President
SARA WELGAN
for
Vice President

Sara Welgan was a good choice on John's part. She was smart and pretty and was a math tutor after school. So she was well known among the student body.

And:

Vote for the WRIGHT Candidate!
Anthony Wright for School President
Hailey Jones for Vice President

They were everywhere, and people were really starting to buzz about them. Anthony had the brilliant idea to put a photo of himself and Hailey on his poster, which gave them an identity boost immediately. I heard kids saying, "Oh, *that*'s Anthony Wright," as they looked at the posters in the hall. I was happy to see that they'd used my line in his poster too. Writing talent was certainly useful in a campaign, but more behind the scenes than in front, I guess.

Hailey was in her element too, as it turned out. It reminded me of the Dear Know-It-All letter from College Reject and my feelings about spending time doing what you love being good for your soul. Hailey was actually blossoming with all the campaigning. She was jazzed and talking a mile a minute about what she and Anthony could do to help the school. I was really impressed—and proud. She'd stand outside the cafeteria at lunch and hand out leaflets about their campaign platform and some of their ideas. Anthony had embraced all of Hailey's ideas and worked a few of them into his materials in a seamless way. They were an unlikely team, but they actually complemented each other really well. I was psyched for both of them.

But Tuesday afternoon, when Hailey came over to do homework with me, she was upset.

"What's wrong?" I said when I answered the door and saw the tears streaming down her face.

She wailed, "Everyone's teasing me about the centipede!"

"Whaaaat?"

She pulled away and nodded. "Everyone keeps saying, 'Eek!' when they see me." She sniffled dramatically.

I fought off a smile that was trying to bloom on my face. "Oh, Hails," I said sympathetically.

"I'll never live it down!" she cried, and flopped on the couch.

I sat down next to her and thought hard. Then I said, "Hailey, I know what to do. Sit up. Listen."

She sat up and rolled her eyes, but she listened.

"You need to embrace it. You need to style yourself a Centipede Warrior. You need to laugh when kids say 'Eek!' to you. It's the only way. Otherwise you become a victim. Get it?"

Hailey was quiet for a minute. Then she sighed heavily. "Whatever. I'm such a loser. Anthony

Wright should get rid of me while he still can. I'll bring him down."

"Hailey! Don't be a wimp; be a warrior! Come on! It's up to you how you handle it. Now, let's go get a snack and you'll feel better, okay?"

By the end of our homework session, I was pretty sure I'd convinced Hailey to be a Centipede Warrior, but you never know with her; she could change in an instant. At the door, when she was leaving, I made a fist, pumped it at her, and said, "Battle on, Warrior!" and she did kind of smile. I was trying to do a little campaign management of my own, but it wasn't clear if it was working. Maybe I'd made some progress. Maybe.

★   ★   ★

I got my own homework out of the way and then attacked the Anthony Wright article again. I was striving to be as objective as I could, with the new added complication that my best friend was Anthony's running mate. I struggled over the paragraph devoted to Hailey, trying to strike the right balance between selling her hard and staying neutral. I also worked hard to keep the mugger story small (Anthony hadn't even wanted me to mention it) and concrete plans for the school front and center. I stopped for a quick dinner with my mom; Allie was out at a meeting with Anthony and wouldn't be home for dinner. I felt good about having put those two together, and I knew she'd really help. With the speeches only three days away, their work was cut out for them.

When I finally felt I'd done as much as I could on the Wright article, I printed it out and laid it on my bed to put in my messenger bag for my meeting with Michael; then I turned to my Dear Know-It-All letter response.

I felt I'd actually learned even more this week that I could put into the response, especially after confronting my choice of running for office versus staying on the paper, and listening to Anthony talk about how far his extracurriculars had taken him. As I sat at my desk in front of my computer, the letter lying beside me, I thought about how the choices we make at an early age actually matter. Maybe not in terms of the outcome, but in terms of learning how to make choices and learning that it can be hard to choose—especially when friends are involved.

Naturally, as I held my fingers above the keyboard to start my reply, my door swung open and Allie was there with her cheeks flushed and her eyes shining. I moved to hide the Dear Know-It-All letter, but she was so excited, she didn't even notice this time.

"What's up?" I asked.

"I think he's going to win!" she cried, and she sat down happily on my bed.

"You do? Why? How?"

"We were at the Java Stop and lots of kids were coming up to Anthony and saying hi and stuff. I think people are figuring out who he is. It's kind of like a grassroots thing."

"Cool! Did you get a sense of where they know him from?"

Allie thought for a second. "Well, one guy said he recognized Anthony from the posters. Another girl was in his homeroom but hadn't realized he was running. Three kids read about him on Buddybook and wanted to hear all about the mugging and how he won the giant chess trophy they have at school. I put a picture of that on his Buddybook page," she said with a proud smile.

"That's great, Al! I've got a really good article on him too. I can't wait for it to run."

Allie clapped her hands together. "Awesome! Can I see it?"

I paused for a minute. "Um, it's not really done yet. I mean . . ." I happened to glance at the article lying next to her on the bed. Darn it! I was usually so cautious about her finding my Dear Know-It-All stuff that I'd never thought to bother hiding a regular news article.

Allie followed my glance with narrowed eyes and then pounced on the article next to her.

"Aha!" she said.

I sighed heavily and waited for her to finish. Watching her face, I saw her smile, nod, frown a little, bite her lip, and then, as she finished, she grew angry. She laid the article back on the bed with an icy coldness. She folded her hands in her lap and looked at me.

"What?" I said innocently.

"Is that really the best you can do, Sam?" she said in an angry voice.

"What are you talking about? I think it's very well written!"

"I don't care how it's written," said Allie. "I care what it says, and it does not say enough about how great our candidate is!"

"Okay, hang on a second," I said. "Anthony is not 'our' candidate. He certainly has my vote, but I am not working on his campaign and I don't have any vested interest in whether or not he wins. I have a job to do, and that is to report the news fairly and accurately, with absolutely no bias! And that's what I've done! Do you want to get me fired from the paper?"

"I just think you should have made more of his heroics—the chess wins, the mugging incident . . ."

"Allie, Anthony asked me not to even write about that! He's embarrassed by it! He doesn't want to be a hero, and he also doesn't want people knowing he lives in a sketchy neighborhood where people can still get mugged!"

Allie looked at me with her eyes blazing. "I don't care what Anthony wants! I'm the one who knows how to promote him! I know how to get him elected!"

"Whoa! Listen to yourself. This is out of control! It's a school election. I know you love this stuff, but seriously, chillax!"

Allie was breathing fast, but I think I was getting through to her.

"Seriously!" I said again, shaking my head. I wondered if this is how real political journalists feel sometimes.

Politics Too Dirty, Journo Retires to Sports Pages.

"Okay. Okay. Right." Allie put her hands on her knees and pushed herself up and off my bed. "Fine. I get it." She left my room in a daze, I guess trying to figure out what had happened to her to make her so nuts.

I shook my head and stood up to put the article in my messenger bag, as I should have right from the start. Then I sat back at my desk to draft my response to College Reject.

Dear College Applicant,

First of all, I refuse to refer to you as "College Reject Already," since you aren't.

Second of all, you are right. But so are your parents.

You are right because you should be spending time on what you love and not doing activities or pursuing hobbies just because they'll get you into college one day. Colleges can smell a phony a mile away, and they can also spot someone who's really unhappy with how they spend their time. It's the people who are passionate they get excited about; it doesn't matter what the passion is for as much as how hard you work at it and how it feeds your soul. More important, no one in middle school should make themselves miserable spending time on stuff they don't enjoy. (Not counting homework, of course!)

Now, this is where your parents are right: It's a good idea to have something you love and work hard at. It will get you places in life, like into college or elected school president or something. Just work as hard as you can at the things you love most, whether it's sports, reading, or playing chess. Don't worry so much about the payoff on the other end. If you are excited and try hard, things will fall into place for you. You'll just naturally pick up skills that will take you places in life. I'm sure of it.

Good luck with seventh grade, and don't forget to vote on Monday!

Signed,

Know-It-All

I read it and reread it and made a few small corrections, but mostly I was happy with it. I'd considered Anthony and Hailey, me and Michael as I'd written it. Maybe our passions— journalism, politics, sports—wouldn't lead to Ivy League colleges, but they'd given us lots of great experiences and good times so far. I knew that would pay off one way or another someday. I attached it to an e-mail and sent it off to Mr. Trigg. I hoped he'd like it.

I ran into Allie in the hall, and she seemed to have calmed down a little. She was brushing her teeth, and she stared at me for a moment, not saying anything. I was quiet as well, and so the only sound was Allie's toothbrush swishing back and forth.

"I just want him to win," she finally said through a mouthful of toothpaste.

"I know. I do too. And I'm not even supposed to say that," I said.

She nodded and kept brushing, but I knew we were at peace now.

Chapter 10

GIRL BURSTS AWAITING COMPLIMENT

★ ★ ★

Michael and I met after school on Wednesday and walked to Slices, where we had a snack and swapped articles to edit. It was comfortable reading in silence next to him, but I did sneak a couple of peeks to see if he looked like he was enjoying what I'd written. Also because he had on my favorite of his shirts—a faded denim button-down that had belonged to his oldest brother and made his eyes look amazing.

Once he caught me looking, and I quickly looked back down at what I was reading, though I know my eyes swam over the page since I'd lost track of where I was.

"Paste," he said in a cautioning tone.

I looked up innocently, and our eyes met.

"Don't you like it?" he asked.

"What? Oh. Yes, of course. It's great. I was just trying to see if you liked mine."

He nodded. "It's very good. Very objective." I'd told him about Allie, so I smiled at the reference. We both looked back at the articles in earnest and finished reading.

His article about John Scott covered all the basics about John's life, his activities, his family, and his background in general. Though it was very detailed and well written, it felt bland, and I flashed back to this issue's Dear Know-It-All letter, suddenly wondering if John's parents were behind his run or if it was all him. He suddenly seemed so . . . packaged. In contrast, my article really gave a sense of who Anthony Wright was, where he was coming from and why, and most of all, that it was all his. His ideas, his drive, his motivation, his experience. I don't want to toot my own horn, but my article was better. Not the writing, but the subject matter, for sure.

"Well?" said Michael.

"You first," I said, taking a careful sip of my soda. I really, really hoped he liked mine.

Girl Bursts Awaiting Compliment.

"Okay. He has my vote," he said with a chuckle.

"Oh no! It's not supposed to be an endorsement!" I sighed and slapped the table hard with my hand in frustration.

Michael shook his head as he sipped his soda, too. "It doesn't read like one. Anthony sells himself. I actually kind of agree with Allie. I can see why she was annoyed. You almost bend over backward to *not* sell him."

"Uh-oh. Now I feel bad the other way," I said.

"Don't! You did the right thing. I made a couple of little corrections and suggestions, but overall, I think it's almost perfect. Great job, Pasty. Again." He grinned. "Now, what did you think of mine?"

"Great writing, great reporting, I love how you worked in the man-on-the-streets, the Buddybook poll info. Actually, it's interesting, because in person, John's amazing, but on paper . . ."

"He wilts," admitted Michael, nodding.

I nodded back.

Michael sighed hard and put his face in his hands in a gesture of exhaustion. Then he looked up at me again. "I tried. I *really* tried hard to make him come alive on the page. The problem is, there's no *there* there. No backstory, no life challenges, no passionate hobbies. The drowning thing looks lame when you spell it all out. And the campaign promises . . ." He sighed again in aggravation. "New team uniforms, iPads, gourmet lunches, less homework? It all sounds like . . . fantasy!"

I sighed in agreement. "I know. I like how you handled that, though. 'The *Cherry Valley Voice* staff will be interested in hearing specifically how John intends to follow through on his promises.' Good one. But this is still tough."

We looked at each other, our mouths in identical grim lines.

"What can we do?" I asked finally.

Michael shrugged. "I'm just worried that the contrast in the profiles will make it seem like we're not being objective. Like we're really selling Anthony and not John. And I do feel bad about that."

I nodded. "It's so funny, because I think we were worried at the beginning that it would be the opposite problem, right?"

Michael nodded vigorously. "For sure. John is so good in person. I thought he'd be the clear winner."

"What should we do?" I asked.

Michael thought for a minute; then he said, "I think we just go home, make the corrections, and e-mail them to Trigger. Let's ask him what he thinks."

★ ★ ★

Hailey IM'd me that night.

Trying to be a warrior. It's tougher than I thought. Kind of getting better at it.

I smiled and wrote back.

You already are. You just need to remember it.

Still smiling, I saw an e-mail come into my in-box, and I clicked over to see what it was. It was from Mr. Trigg, addressed to me and Michael both. It said:

Please stop in to see me first thing tomorrow.

—PT

I forwarded it to Michael with just a question mark, and he replied with the same. Was Mr. Trigg mad? Happy? There was no way to know. I slept uneasily all night, worried that my career at the *Cherry Valley Voice* might be over.

Journalists Fired on Eve of Election.

Gulp. Would he do that?

★   ★   ★

Thursday morning, Michael and I met at my locker and hustled wordlessly to the newsroom. Mr. Trigg was in his office, brewing tea, of course, and reading yet another well-thumbed book about Winston Churchill.

"Ah, my star political reporting team! Come in. Do come in! Fancy a cup of tea, do you?"

Exchanging a nervous glance, we declined and leaned awkwardly in Mr. Trigg's office doorway. He arranged his own tea, took a sip, and pulled up our articles on his screen, side by side. Then he made his hands into a tepee shape and tapped them against his lips as he thought. Michael and I exchanged a nervous glance. Where was this all going?

Finally Mr. Trigg spoke. "Same word count, almost. Same number of paragraphs. Identical column inches. Was that intentional?"

Michael and I looked at each other again. "No," said Michael.

"Well done, then," said Mr. Trigg.

Michael and I raised our eyebrows at each other.

"I can see your predicament," said Mr. Trigg after another pause. "And now, *my* predicament. I don't think . . . I really think there's nothing we can do. Sometimes things just become very clear when you write about them. Maybe . . . certainly, I could run the Scott article above the fold, a little more prominently? Even things up that way? But no. That's not right either. That would look like an endorsement too." He sighed heavily and looked up at us. "I think you've really done your best, you know? We just run them and see what happens. Of course, there will be the speeches tomorrow, and that should take some heat off you. The speeches are always the biggest deciding factor. But, of course, we've never had a candidate with such an interesting backstory before."

Michael and I both sagged a little in relief. We weren't in trouble. We were Mr. Trigg's coworkers, trying to solve an editorial problem.

"So we're not in trouble?" said Michael, slightly joking but serious, I knew.

Mr. Trigg looked up at us in alarm. "Trouble? Certainly not! Why would you be in trouble?"

"Because we weren't objective enough?" I said.

"Ms. Martone, if you'd been any more objective . . . why, I think I would've said you were against Anthony Wright!" He chuckled.

I rolled my eyes. "I've heard that before."

Mr. Trigg clapped his hands and stood up. "No. There's nothing more to be done but run it and let nature take its course. That's all we can do."

"Okay, thanks," I said, still nervous. Part of me was glad I wasn't the one who'd had to write the John Scott article.

★   ★   ★

The *Cherry Valley Voice* hit the Web just after midnight that night, and the hard copies were being distributed by sixth graders at the front door to school as usual. I stood back and watched as people eagerly took copies—did this many people usually take a copy?—and began reading the candidate profiles on the front page immediately.

I was dreading the day. I was nervous about reactions to our articles, nervous about reactions to my Dear Know-It-All column, and really, really nervous about the speeches. I knew it was going to be a challenge for Anthony, and I really, really wanted him to win. Allie was even taking the afternoon off to come and prep him and watch. She'd gotten special permission from her guidance counselor.

Finally I steeled myself against the day and entered the school, grabbing a hard copy of the paper (even though I'd read it online as soon as I got up this morning), more to hide behind if need be.

Inside, everyone was chatting about the paper, the speeches, the election. There were more posters on the wall than ever, and Anthony and

John were both in the main hall, handing out flyers again while Hailey scurried to replenish Anthony's supply. I slunk to my locker, hoping to avoid conversation, and I nearly managed it until I saw Michael's friend Frank Duane walking in the hall.

"Hey, Sam! What gives with the articles? Why so hard on the candidates?"

I shrugged. "Oh, did you think we were hard on them?"

Frank nodded. "Yeah. John Scott's a great guy, and he comes off like a dud. And Anthony Wright . . . do you like the guy?"

I cringed. "Love him," I said, and Frank laughed.

"Oh, right. I saw the photo on Buddybook. I almost forgot!" He walked away, chuckling.

Darn it!

The day continued in that vein, with some people actually mad at me that I hadn't written more strongly in favor of Anthony or Michael in favor of John. *Writers Buffeted by Stormy Election Coverage Seek Shelter.*

By the time I found Michael at lunch, I felt like I'd been doing battle all day. He had the same worn-out look to him.

"Bad day?" I asked as I put my tray down.

"Terrible," he said, brushing his hair off his forehead in frustration.

"How's that plan to be a political journalist going so far?" I teased.

"Not going. That would be a nightmare. I'm thinking of switching to fashion coverage."

I laughed darkly and nodded. "Though Jeff Perry's certainly well on his way to a career in political photography."

Now it was Michael's turn to laugh.

"Want to sit together at the speeches?" he asked.

"Yes. Are we there to report or just as civilians?"

"I imagine the next issue of the paper will have to contain something about the speeches, but with the election coming on Monday, it'll just be a small part of the story about who won."

I nodded, my stomach filled with butterflies. "I hope that's a happy headline."

★　　★　　★

At two thirty, the whole school converged on the auditorium. It was packed.

"People, if we could just clear a path through the aisles for safety . . . ," Mr. Pfeiffer was saying into a bullhorn. Kids were sitting everywhere—on the floor, around the edges of the stage, on laps, in the aisles. It was mayhem. I was lucky I'd had gotten out of my last class early, since we'd finished a project and the teacher knew we were dying to get to the auditorium. I'd been able to rush in and save prime seats for me, Allie, and Michael. Hailey and Anthony would sit onstage in chairs reserved for them and Sara and John.

Eventually, Michael arrived, and pretty soon after, Mr. Pfeiffer got everyone quieted down. Then the candidates walked in and it was chaos all over again. People were cheering, stomping, whistling. I couldn't believe it. It took ten minutes of calming everyone down before John could even get up to speak. I was glad he was going first because I knew he'd be good, and I hoped that would help Anthony calm down and see how he'd survive.

John stood at the podium, perfectly comfortable,

chuckling and enjoying it all. He was a natural politician, I could see. He ate up the attention and felt perfectly at ease in this role. But when he started to talk, he lost me. Sure, he was great: funny, charming, handsome, full of incredible promises and ideas. If I didn't know better, I'd say instantly that he had my vote. I only hoped everyone in the audience would listen closely and hear how empty his promises were, how pie-in-the-sky. And I hoped they'd keep their ears open to hear what Anthony had to say after.

When John finished, Sara joined him at the podium and he introduced her. They left the stage to incredible cheering, clapping, and so on, again. After what seemed like an eternity, it was Anthony's turn.

My palms were soaking wet as I watched Anthony stand. He had a notebook in his hands, and I prayed it was just a prop and that he wouldn't read his speech word for word. He turned and reached one hand out to Hailey. She stood with him, and they both walked to the podium.

Cheering, clapping, stomping—there was lots

of it. Not as much as for John, but Anthony wasn't as much of a known quantity, so I wasn't worried yet. I could see Anthony was nervous, though, and so was Hailey. They stood there, smiling, and then it happened.

"Eeek!"

I heard the first one.

"Eeek! *Eeek!* Eeek!"

Suddenly the whole crowd was "Eek"-ing.

"O-M-G!" I turned first to Michael, who was looking shocked, then Allie, whose face had completely fallen. She was ash-white. Then I looked back at Hailey, whose mouth was open in a small O. What would she do? How would Anthony handle it?

Oh no!

Would the headline for the next issue of the Cherry Valley Voice be:

Candidates Collapse Onstage from Nerves Election Eve?

Chapter 11

TRAINING PAYS OFF IN UNDERDOG RACE

★ ★ ★

The crowd fell silent for an awkward second or two as a few more "Eeks" rang out. Mr. Pfeiffer stood up from his chair, put his folder down, and began to cross the stage to take charge.

But then Anthony smiled widely and said, "I can see you've met my vice president, Hailey Jones, the Centipede Warrior!"

There was a brief pause, and then the place went wild.

"Hailey! Hailey! Hailey! Hailey!" they chanted. People cheered and yelled and stomped and applauded and whistled—way louder than anything they'd done for John and Sara.

"Come on, Hails," I whispered. "You can handle this!" I crossed my fingers and my toes and held my breath, praying she'd react appropriately.

And finally, Hailey stepped forward, grinned a huge grin, and waved at the crowd. I breathed a massive sigh of relief. Hailey then settled the crowd down and said, "I'd like to introduce the next school president, the Wright choice, Anthony Wright!"

By the time Anthony even started his speech, he'd basically won. But the speech was excellent anyway. He talked about his childhood, how much the school meant to him, what he hoped to do and why, and, most important, how. He was specific and smart and even funny a few times, but most of all he sounded serious, reliable, and trustworthy. It was clear he was up there for the "right" reasons (ha-ha), and not just because he wanted to win or because it would look good on his college applications one day.

When I looked at Allie halfway through, her face was glowing even though her arms were tightly crossed in front of her chest and she had one fist in a ball up by her mouth. Turning to Michael, I whispered, "They're gonna win."

He nodded and smiled, unable to tear his eyes away from Anthony.

Training Pays Off in Underdog Race.

Afterward, Michael, Allie, and I fought the crowds to say congratulations to Hailey and Anthony. They were laughing and happy, just so relieved it was over.

Allie grabbed Anthony in a big hug. "You did it! You nailed it!"

"Thanks to you, Coach!"

"Great job, guys," I said with a proud smile.

While Anthony and Michael shook hands, I whispered to Hailey, "You did it. It was you. I'm so proud!"

She smiled back. "I guess sometimes you've just gotta go with the flow and embrace the teasing, right, Pasty?"

I grinned. "Right."

Just then, who should come along to congratulate Hailey but Gregory Toms, the originator of "Eek, a mouse!" I could see Hailey struggling with whether to be mad at him for starting it or happy to see him, and the happiness won out. After all, the "Eek" thing had been good in the end. It gave them an identity. And Gregory was pretty darn cute!

I decided to give them some privacy, but as I turned to walk away, Anthony grabbed my shoulder. "Hey, Sam. I just wanted to say thanks. Whatever ends up happening Monday, either way, I feel like today was a victory. I had the chance to get my ideas out there, and also, just being able to get up there and talk in front of so many people was great. I never dreamed it would go so well. And I couldn't have done it without you. You brought Allie and Hailey to me and also wrote the nice article. I just really appreciate it."

"It was my pleasure. I'd love to see you guys win on Monday. It would be great for the school. You have my vote!" I said, and I laughed. "As if you didn't know that!"

"Well, thanks." And just then Anthony's mom and some of his siblings bustled up onstage, laughing about how hard it had been to get down the aisle through the crowds, and I left them alone to enjoy their congratulations.

Jumping off the stage, I motioned to Allie that I'd meet her outside; then I started walking away.

"Paste!"

Michael caught up, and we headed out together. I couldn't have been happier.

"Hey, there's a new movie out I think I heard you wanted to see. Something about England in the olden days?"

I looked at him to see if he was teasing me, but he wasn't laughing.

"Yeah? And?"

"Wanna go see it this weekend, like, if you're not too busy?"

I paused. This was pretty date-ish. "Uh, are there going to be centipedes there, because . . ."

And we started to laugh.

★   ★   ★

Hailey and Anthony won by a mile on Monday. The election wasn't even close, and I felt a little bad for John Scott. The Wright team made a plan for a big dinner celebration at Anthony's house. My mom was going to bring me and Allie and Hailey, and then Hailey's dad would bring us home after. I couldn't wait.

After school I packed all my candidate research materials into files, pulling the relevant notebook pages out and stuffing them in too. I'd decide to give it all to Mr. Trigg. You never know, one day a reporter might come calling to see what we have on those two. I'm sure they'll be big successes in one arena or another.

As I sorted the papers, an IM appeared on my screen. It was from Michael. We'd had a great time Saturday, turning it into a big group outing instead of "just the two of us" date. And the funny thing was, I was happy about it. Spending time with Michael is all that matters, and honestly, I'm just not sure I'm ready to do a one-on-one non-working date with him. So Hailey and Anthony came, and Kristen and Frank. It was fun. We went to Slices after, and Anthony cracked everyone up with his flawless imitations of an English accent; then Michael took me home.

His IM now said:

Going to the party?

I smiled and typed back.

Of course. You?

There was a pause and then:

Yup. Ran into John Scott, and he's all excited

about starting a rock band. Said it's what he's always wanted to do. Can u believe?

Huh. That was interesting. I sat back and thought for a minute before I typed my reply.

Why?

Then I waited.

Something about Dear Know-It-All and his parents' dreams. Who knows with that guy?

No way! I grinned. Then I typed.

That Dear Know-It-All sure knows his stuff.

There was a really long pause, and then Michael wrote back.

She sure does.

Extra! Extra!

Want the scoop on what Samantha is up to next?

Here's a sneak peek of the tenth book in the Dear Know-It-All series:

Breaking News

FOOTBALL SEASON BEGINS; MARTONE FALLS FOR STAR QUARTERBACK

If you're a fact-loving person like I am, you probably think superstitions are a little silly. So tell me, why does it seem like *everyone* believes in them? Take my mom, for instance. You would think that a freelance accountant, a person who works with numbers all day, would know that there's nothing particularly special or spooky about the number thirteen. Except that every time the calendar shows a big black thirteen on a Friday, Mom gets an uneasy look in her eye. It's like she's waiting for something really bad to happen. Of course nothing does, just like nearly every other day of the year!

As a journalist, my instincts are to get to the truth of the matter. So I started Googling, and I found some interesting information about "friggatriskaidekaphobia." (That's the actual term for the condition of the fear of Friday the thirteenth. And I dare you to say that three times fast!) Did you know that in Spanish-speaking countries, it's Tuesday the thirteenth that's considered unlucky? And in Italy, Friday the seventeenth is the day of doom. I figure that kind of info will come in handy when I'm traveling the world on assignment as an investigative reporter.

But the next step on my career path is to continue to build my reputation as star reporter of the *Cherry Valley Voice*, our school newspaper. Of course, I don't usually fly solo. Mr. Trigg likes to give the best articles to his dream team, his "Woodward and Bernstein," as he calls Michael Lawrence and me, after the *Washington Post*'s legendary reporting duo. I'm not sure we'll ever get behind the scenes at the White House, but we did write the story that revealed the truth about our class president contenders.

Not that I'm complaining about sharing the glory. Not one teensy bit. I won't even mind if someday Michael and I get picked to be coeditors in chief. Then I'll get to work side by side with him all the time. I've known Michael since kindergarten, and even though he sometimes annoyingly calls me Pasty (you eat paste one time when you're five and you're branded forever!), he's still the only boy I've ever dreamed of calling my boyfriend.

How can I describe Michael Lawrence's insane cuteness to you? Let's just say that if you took the hottest member of every boy band, mixed up all of their best qualities in a pot, and then increased them to the tenth power, well, then you'd have Michael Lawrence. It's actually shocking that he hasn't been discovered yet.

So back to superstitions: I don't have many, being a believer in cold, hard facts, but I do have a lucky green T-shirt. (Its luck is based on the fact that it is the exact same shade of green as my eyes.) Maybe it's not really lucky, but it does make me really happy. I put it on with a long, hippy skirt and green UGGS. I wrapped a sparkly beaded scarf around my neck. Then I threw on an armful of bangle bracelets and some beaded hanging earrings for a little extra pizzazz. I looked in the mirror. "Not bad, Martone," I thought to myself.

But the real proof waited across the hallway. I knocked on my sister Allie's door. Allie can be a real pain because she's always creeping around my stuff, but she does have much better fashion sense than I do.

"What do you think?" I asked as I warily entered her room.

Allie glanced up from her texting for exactly one one-hundredth of a second and rolled her eyes. "No," she huffed, obviously revolted by my choice of apparel. "Just no."

"But it's my lucky shirt," I explained.

"Lucky because you're going to fold it up and put it back in your drawer," Allie said bluntly. "And that scarf? That jewelry? You do realize you're going to a football game, right?"

Allie took my hand and led me back into my room the way she used to drag me across the street when I was too little to cross by myself. She opened my closet door and started picking out items and throwing them onto my bed.

"Allie, I don't have a lot of time to try on clothes," I complained. "Hailey will be here any minute!"

"This won't take long," Allie said. "Just listen. You're the starting QB's girlfriend. You have to look great, but not like you're trying too hard. Think casual chic."

"I'm not Michael Lawrence's girlfriend!" I said, automatically. Well, I didn't think I was. But I'd like to be.

"Whatever," Allie snorted. "Just take my advice."

I looked at the clock, and my stomach started to hurt. How could getting dressed for a football game be so incredibly painful?

"Try this," Allie said as she tossed some clothes my way.

I quickly pulled on some black leggings and then a miniskirt. Next came a gray tank, followed by a silver sweater and a black blazer. A pair of old-school black high-top sneakers finished the outfit. I looked in the mirror and smiled. I looked very casual and comfy but very stylish, too. Allie was amazing—the outfit worked like a lucky charm. Just in time, too.

"SAAAAMMMM!" I heard Hailey call from the front door.

"COMMMINNNGGGG!" I yelled back. "Thanks, Allie!" I called behind me, but she had already started texting again.

I raced down the stairs (without tripping!) and stopped to say good-bye to my mom. She was in her home office, intently focused on some confusing jumble of budget numbers.

"You look great," she said.

"Thanks," I answered. "Go, Cherry Valley!"

"Go, Cherry Valley?" Hailey said from behind my back. "More like Go, Sam! Supercute outfit!"

"Yeah, it was Allie's creation," I said.

"She got her fashion sense from me," Mom said, not even kidding.

We raced out of the house and jumped into the backseat of Hailey's car. Hailey's dad turned around and pretended to tip his hat.

"Good evening, mademoiselles," he said in a fake accent. "Where shall I be driving you this fine afternoon?"

Hailey and I just looked at each other and

started to giggle uncontrollably. Parents. Did they even have a clue how embarrassing they could be?

"Football field, Dad," Hailey answered as soon as she had regained her composure. "Pronto."

★　　★　　★

It took only seven minutes to get from my house to the football field, but in that short period of time, Hailey bombarded me with at least ten thousand questions. Did Michael say anything about hanging out with you after the game? Do you think the guys from the team will go to Scoops? Should we go, too? What if they have a bad game? Do you know if that cute guy from West Hills plays football? Do you think he has a girlfriend?

"Hailey, stop!" I said. "We're just going to a football game. The rest we'll improvise. Okay?"

"Okay." Hailey laughed. "I have just one last question for you, Samantha Martone." She held up her hand to my face like she was holding a microphone. "Will . . . you . . . touch . . . ," she asked, sounding like the most dramatic sports reporter ever, " . . . the cougar?"

We both started giggling uncontrollably.

"Yes, I guess I will," I confessed. "I'll bow to peer pressure and silly superstition."

"It's not silly," Hailey said. "It's tradition. And really, really bad luck if you don't."

Let me explain. There's a statue of a cougar standing on its hind legs in front of Cherry Valley Middle School. All of our sports teams are named the Cougars, and like a million years ago, some class raised enough money to have the statue built and installed in front of the school. Hailey's soccer team, Michael's baseball and football teams, bowling, tennis, they're all Cougars.

Cherry Valley legend says that if you rub the cougar's paw, you'll have good luck. Everyone at Cherry Valley Middle School seems to believe this myth—students, parents, teachers, even Principal Pfeiffer. Kids rub Mr. Cougar's paw before a big test, when they're going to ask someone to a school dance, and of course, before every sporting event. The paw has been rubbed so many times over the years that it is as smooth and shiny as glass.

When we turned the last corner, I felt a little flutter in my stomach. Even though Michael Lawrence is definitely not my boyfriend—yet—it was going to be fun to cheer for him. I looked out the window and started to daydream. The clear blue skies, the red and yellow leaves that swirled in the wind, the crisp chill in the air—it was the perfect setting for a girl reporter to walk home hand in hand with the triumphant quarterback after the game. *Ace Reporter Spotted with All-Star QB!*

"Sam!" Hailey said, a little too loudly considering we were sitting right next to each other. "What do you think is going on?"

It took me a second to realize what Hailey was talking about. She pointed out her window at the front of our school. A large crowd was gathered.

Then we spotted the police car. This was definitely not a pregame pep rally. I glanced at Hailey, and she looked as nervous as I felt. Why would the police be at a middle school football game?

"You two stay here while I make sure everything's okay," Hailey's dad said.

Hailey and I held hands until her dad waved us over. And then we finally saw what all the commotion was about.

It was Mr. Cougar. His paw was on the ground, smashed into tiny pieces. His body was covered with a spray-painted message: **CV—Your Luck Has Run Out.** Police were wrapping yellow caution tape around the statue. Lots of people were taking pictures of the vandalized property. It seemed like a scene from a movie, not like something that would happen in our town.

Hailey gasped. "Cherry Valley Middle School is doomed."

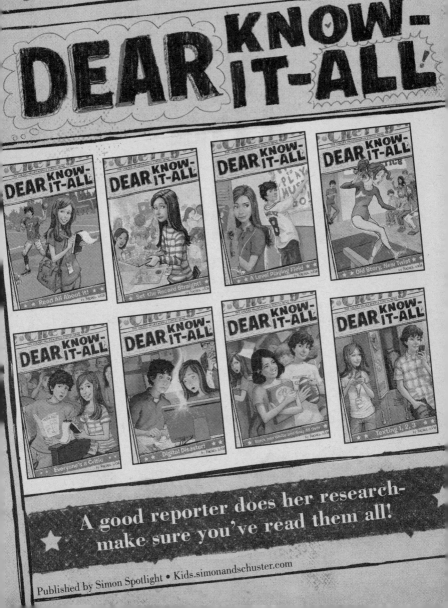